I0727000

TUATHA

Morgan Silas Donnelly

Tales of the People Series
Book 1

Copyright © 2025 by Morgan Silas Donnelly.

All rights reserved. No part of this book may be reproduced or used in any manner without written permission of the copyright owner except for the use of quotations in a book review. For more information, contact: writer@morgansilasdonnelly.com.

ISBN Paperback: # 978-1-7382574-7-8
ISBN Electronic: # 978-1-7382574-8-5

Original Artwork: Talia Cook - @taliscolortouch
Publishing Consultant: PRESStinely - PRESStinely.com

This book is a work of fiction. The names, characters, and events in this book are the products of the author's imagination or are used fictitiously. Any similarity to real persons, living or dead, is coincidental and not intended by the author.

All original stories written by Morgan Silas Donnelly. The Shipwreck was previously published in Whispers of the Deep, © 2025 Tiny Gnat Publishing and is used by permission.

Morgan Silas Donnelly
Tiny Gnat Publishing

MorganSilasDonnelly.com

Table of Contents

Prologue

I'm talking again with the girl who tells stories of long-ago friendships. You will meet her later in the book, for she has her own story to tell.

"Oh, do we have fun, Morgan! I met you in a playground of sorts—I and all the other characters you've written! We all have stories, we all have dreams, we all have inspirations to live up to. We, the characters you write about in your fables and parables, have dealt with themes of segregation, advancement, community, expansive love, empowerment, generational healing, family, conflict, and rebuilding society.

"We, the characters of this book, and you, yourself, Morgan, all love playing and communicating deep thematic verse.

"It is a pleasure to meet you, dear reader, for sharing is truly a form of caring. In sharing is the start of community, and that is one of the deepest forms of love, although humans don't yet realize that.

"Our prologue is our welcome, and our closing to this prologue is the request that you one day share your story too, dear reader, for stories help build community. That is all for now."

The Caterpillar

There is a caterpillar up in a tree branch munching away happily on the plentiful leaves, living her best life. She looks slightly cartoonish, with large eyes and a beautiful plump green body glistening with the remnants of morning dew, as the sun rapidly rises.

A robin comes along. He perches next to this caterpillar and exclaims, "I would like to eat you!"

The caterpillar ignores the interruption and continues on her way. She munches some more, and then she says, "No, that would not be a good idea."

The robin looks around perplexed, trying to understand why it would not be a good idea for a bird to eat an insect. He cocks his head this way and that way at the strange notion that eating a bug could ever be a bad idea.

"So tell me then, caterpillar, what should I do with you?"

"You can sit and talk if you like, or you can fly away, or you can go back to your nest. There are many things for you to do. There are worms on the ground in plain sight of here if you are hungry!" she says.

"Ah," the robin roars, "the worms are there on the ground, but you are here, and I am here, and my tummy is rumbling!"

"Hmmm." The caterpillar thinks on that a moment while she chews some food. "I would be most disagreeable in your stomach," she finally says.

The robin looks around to see if she's talking to someone else with these outrageous words! The robin declares, "But I am a bird, and you are a caterpillar, and this time, it is time to eat!" as he moves forward with his beak open and ready.

"No. I don't think so," the caterpillar replies quite calmly. "I am happy here on my branch, eating leaves. I have a change to make. I am important. I have a date to keep."

"Oh," says the robin as he stops his advance and takes a step backwards at this revelation. "I did not know that." The robin shrugs his wings and moves as if to fly away. He then pauses and thinks for a moment before saying out loud, "I am still hungry. Come let me eat you!"

The caterpillar who has by now moved off of her first leaf and has already started eating at another leaf continues to munch, continues to do her caterpillar things, for she is right. There is a change coming for her.

"Would you stop?" she replies to the robin without looking at him at all. "Would you stop the hands of time? Would you drain the beaches of their sand? Would you blow out all the stars in the night sky?" She looks at him as she resumes munching on this new leaf, her last meal.

Again, he is taken aback, and he looks around, and he says, "Well, no. Of course not. That would be silly to do those things."

"Then it would be silly," the caterpillar replies right away, "to eat me as well, for I am not the clock ticking away, and I am not a grain of sand, nor am I a star in the sky, but I am just as important, and it is my duty to get to my destined place to do what I must in this life."

The robin takes another step back as he peers at her intently. "Oh," is all he says.

Our friend the caterpillar continues to munch her leafy meal. The robin paces back and forth a little bit as he debates what to do.

"She is right," he reasons to himself by muttering out loud. "There are worms in the ground. There are other bugs to eat who are not going to talk me out of eating them by talking at all! And yet she would be a very filling and good-tasting meal for me. I should grab her while she is at her plumpest and most delicious!" He steels his determination, and he strides over to her once again.

"I have decided to eat you anyway!"

The caterpillar remarks, "Oh, that's too bad. I wouldn't want to be you for the next 24 hours!"

The robin again steps back one more time. "Why wouldn't you want to be me for the next day?"

"You will have quite the tummy ache. My change has already begun, and my body is not tasty anymore. It is corpulent, yes, but it is also insalubrious, and I fear it would make you quite sick. Quite sick indeed," she cooly replies between bites of leaf. "No, you should go find another bug."

The robin again cocks his head to one side and looks at her body a little more closely than he had before. "You don't seem that much different than any other caterpillar I have ever eaten."

"The change is on the inside," she says matter of factly to him as she starts to take another bite from yet another leaf. "It's something I can feel and it's something I know. My insides are squishy, and they never were before!

"Don't you ever have feelings? Don't you ever have knowings?" she continues after a moment of thinking. "It's like that. You knew where to build your nest. You knew when the worms would be coming above the ground. You knew many things like when to fly into the mountains and when to fly down by the lake. I know these things but in a different way, and I know that I am not the meal for you."

The robin looks dejectedly downwards. "Yes, that is all true. I do know when to fly south, and when to fly north, and when to fly east, and when to fly west. And I knew how to attract my mate, and I know how to be a good father even now as I argue with an insect who is bonkers."

"Mhhmmm," is all the caterpillar says as she resumes her dining by munching on a fourth leaf now.

The robin looks towards the sun, which has now risen up in the sky from where it was from when he first landed next to a talkative bug. "I will go," he says. "My babies need me, and there is other food to seek. The other food is not changing. Food that is not harmful."

He flies away, looking back at her once. The caterpillar doesn't say anything more at all. She just continues to eat. And when she comes to the last untouched leaf on her branch, she spies a beautiful nesting spot for herself on the next branch up. She crawls up to it and smiles as she starts to spin her silk.

The White Fairy

There once was a fairy. She was a beautiful fairy with white hair, a white dress, white skin, white teeth—she was quite white indeed. She tended a glade in an ancient green forest and she loved being there. A tree-lined stream flowed right through it all.

She tended the trees. She tended the moss. She tended the grass. She tended all of the things that fairies tend. And then, one day, a danger— wildfire—came to her green forest that she called home. She could smell it from a distance. She could see the smoke cloud get larger and larger!

She could feel the fear of the squirrels, and the deer. Even the snakes were afraid! She helped all the creatures of the glade as best she could. "Go this way! Go that way!" she implored. She helped some by saying, "Water is this way." Still others she helped by saying, "It's clear over there. No smoke, no flame, no fire. Go there! Go there!" And she did her best to get everyone out of harm's way.

Her father came into view. "Old Man Forrest" as he was known to some, but he was simply "Papa" to her. Wise beyond his years and wrinkled beyond all hope of anyone ever recognizing the boy he once was.

He urged her to go with him, to move, to leave! To go elsewhere, where the flames were not. And she said, "No, Papa. No, Papa. I need to stay and protect what I can protect and keep safe what I can keep safe."

He replied, "You don't have to help the animals! You can go to safety. This is not your forest. This is my forest and my sacred responsibility."

They held hands for a moment after she held her ground by telling him, "NO!" He departed with a stag, and a doe with a little one in tow. The white fairy stayed and she helped whom she could. She used her magic to bring rain drops down from the sky. The rain was welcome but was not nearly enough to quench the fire. The fire still raged, not caged by her skill.

Her glade burned. Oh, how it burned! She saved the little creatures; yes, she did. But the tall trees, and the green grass, and the low ferns—many were scorched beyond all repair.

When it was done, her father returned from his duties in his very large forest. He looked for her. He called her name. She was there—yes, she was—but she appeared as a shadow.

She was still a fairy, but her home had been burned, so she had been burned. She had been damaged and singed, just like her glade. Her father was vexed that he had left her alone. She said, "It's okay, Papa. All things. All things in time. All things in time, as Momma used to say."

He stayed by her side. He nursed and he nourished her, all the while using his magic on her to support her healing. Her growing strength helped the trees come back, and the grass come back, and the ferns come back too, in the glade that was hers. Her strength was their strength. The stag, and the doe, and her fawn, and the snakes, and the birds, and the squirrels came back too!

And slowly, day by day, Old Man Forrest's daughter became better as she healed. Not quite the same as she was, for now she has a little grey on the edges, instead of all white, but better for all she'd been through. And the forest became alive, as it was not long ago.

The Merchant

The merchant lives in an oasis-blessed city. Only the prepared and equipped go into the wild, for the city is several days' journey inside a hellishly hot, arid desert. The city streets are lined with stone that helps to keep the ever-present fine dust down. The buildings are mud, adobe—the natural material that is all around. There isn't a market square as such in the town, so his small family lives above where he works, as do most people in this city.

His neighbours make a living by selling colourful fabrics, selling food, selling fish—all manner of things that come their way. This merchant, our friend, sells figs, sells dates, sells almonds—things of the land, things that are harvested. He has tables inside and outside of his shop. He sells things that are cared for, things that are tended. He is proud of his wares, and he charges a fair price for a fair day's work.

Late one autumn evening, after dismissing his staff for the day, almost at the hour when he was going to close up the store for the night, a man came by. This man wore a black robe, which matched his black beard, his black eyes, and his black hair. He bought some of the merchant's wares. The stranger paid the agreed price. The merchant got the large order ready and as they were saying goodbye, the merchant noticed the man reach and grab an extra olive.

The theft was subtle. The merchant wondered if perhaps he'd imagined it. He bid the man a good night. He looked down finally and saw that he was indeed low on his olives. He'd had a good day, he reasoned. He had money in his pocket. He was ready to turn in and have dinner with his wife and their one small child, a son.

He brought in his outside tables, closed up the shop and then he went upstairs to have dinner with his family. Evening turned into night turned into morning, and the merchant set up his store again. Passers-by on the street could see his beautiful wares piled high—beautiful almonds, beautiful olives, and such beautiful figs. He said hello to those he knew and welcomed those he didn't. Much later that day, the man with the black robe, black beard, black eyes, and black hair returned. The mystery man bought the same order again!

"You have good service, you have good food, you have good product," said the man by way of small talk. The merchant smiled but was remembering the petty theft so he was not quite as talkative as the day before. He handed the man the order. The man paid a fair price. And again, when they said goodbye, the man reached and got an extra fig this time. The merchant didn't say anything, though the theft was plain to see this time.

The merchant decided to just go about his evening, packing up his store as was his custom. The merchant went upstairs. He kissed his wife, told her about his day, and mentioned the man. He had not mentioned the mystery man the night before. She was intrigued by the mystery of the black robe, black beard, black eyes, and black hair. The wife smiled softly, her way of comforting her husband. She wasn't too concerned about this theft affair because after all, it was only one fig and one olive, and he'd paid a fair price for the two large orders.

The merchant kissed her as a way of acknowledging her wisdom. He, however, still had a feeling in his stomach. He needed to know; he needed to understand why the man was stealing from him. And would the mystery man return tomorrow? Evening turned into night turned into daybreak, and the merchant sprang out of bed to start his day.

He had new stock to put out, things to sort, and employees to yell at, which made him giggle inside. There was much bustle all around, as there was a holiday approaching. Everyone on the market street was getting prepared for it! New banners, new colours, new fabrics—new products—were flowing into the city. The store was so busy, the merchant hardly had time to dwell on the man in the black robe until sure enough, dusk was upon them all, and the man in the black robe returned. This time he only bought figs. The two engaged in a bit of chit chat.

"Different order today?" the merchant asked.

"Yes, a different order for me today," replied the mysterious man.

The man with the black robe, black beard, black eyes, and black hair once again paid a fair price. And yet again, he helped himself to an olive on his way out the door. The merchant had had enough of this man in the black robe, so decided to follow him. He instructed his staff to close up without him. They would know what to do. He could trust them with this.

The streets were crowded even at this hour, but he knew where he was. He could see familiar buildings.

The strange man didn't look around; he just kept going to wherever his destination was. He didn't buy anything else. He seemed to be on a mission. Left turn, right turn, left turn, right turn. Soon the merchant was in an area he didn't know very well. Twilight intensified as the evening wore on.

The man in the black robe knocked on a door and handed a few figs to an old, gnarled woman. A few words were exchanged, and then the man was off to another door, another knock. This time to the door of a stooped older man with white hair—a few figs he gave him. A word passed in departure, then the door closed, and the strange man was off again. Same knock, same quick chat, same giving of figs time and time again. The merchant couldn't understand what the mystery man was doing. Why was the man giving his food away? Why was the man giving away what was his? After all, he'd paid a fair price!

The purloined olive was nowhere to be seen—the merchant wondered about that. More doors, more knocks, more figs dispersed to the elderly and infirm who lived in this slum that the merchant avoided as often as he could. The merchant knew that the bag of figs would soon be empty, so he kept up the game of pretending not to be trailing the man in black, pretending to hide, pretending to fit in where he so obviously didn't. His clothes were quite colourful against the drab and sad buildings in the ever-deepening twilight of the neighbourhood. He fit in less so than the people around him, anyway, with their well-worn and dusty clothes.

Soon, indeed, yes, the bag was empty. The merchant still wondered what had happened to the olive. He soon got his fill of what was to be. The man in black turned yet another corner and came upon the main city square.

There was much sadness. Lepers and amputees and the blind all calling out, "Alms! Alms! A coin for a beggar, sir!" The man in the robe gave none. He said hello instead. He was kind. He encouraged. He knew names, but he did not give coin.

The merchant was just about beside himself now with curiosity and puzzlement. He moved even closer to the mystery man than he had dared be on the streets, wanting to hear what was being said. And the man in black turned around fully this time and said, "Welcome, merchant. How was your day?"

The merchant was surprised, as he thought he was being much stealthier than that! The merchant thought he had been undetected. Alas, he was not.

"I knew you had followed me. What harm would it be to show you?" said the man in black. "Come, I'm sure you're wondering about a certain olive I did not pay for, that was followed the next day by a fig I did not pay for, that was followed this evening by a beautiful olive that is now securely in my robe pocket. One last delivery to make!" The mystery man motioned for the merchant to follow him as he went straight over to a boy, perhaps he was 14 years old, who had jet black hair but not yet a black beard.

The boy was missing his left leg, just after his knee. He stood on crutches. He was dressed in nice clothes, as nice as can be for standing all day outside in the dust and the grime. The boy called out, "Papa, what do you have?" The man in black did not look around.

He presented the olive to his son, the cripple. "It is perfect, yes?"

"Yes, Papa it is. Thank you. Will I see you tomorrow?"

"No, my son. I have business out of town I need to attend to. I'll be gone a few days over the holiday, but I wanted to know you were safe," the now-not-so-mysterious man said gently to his boy.

"I am safe, Papa."

"You can come home, you know. You don't have to live like this."

The boy looked to his left and then replied, "Papa, you know. These are my people. I'm a freak, and they are freaks, in this city of perfection. And us freaks, we get along mostly. I feel like they are family to me. You, and Mama, and my brothers, and sisters, and the wee little ones. You have legs, you have arms, you have eyes. But you don't really see me. You don't really see them, even now, do you, Papa?" as he waved his hand towards the beggars who shared the square with him.

The man swallowed hard and turned away, saying he'd be back again when he could to make sure his son was okay.

The man with his black robe, black beard, black eyes, and black hair went on his way without another word. The merchant watched the man in black depart, then bowed in acknowledgement to the beggar boy before starting on his own way back home to his store. Back home to his family.

He knew the staff would have closed up, and he knew his wife would be worried about him out this late! Sure enough, when he got back home, it was pitch-black dark, punctuated by lanterns in this prosperous part of the city. The store was put away, ready for tomorrow, as he expected it would be.

He went upstairs and discovered his wife was very worried about him.

So he told her a tale of a family's love.

The Princess

I meet a girl as I am walking along a forest path towards a village. The morning sun is just starting to clear the tree tops. The girl is a beautiful and fair princess in a beautiful and fair floor-length dress. It's the old-fashioned kind. The dress, that is, not the girl. The dress has a puff of fabric at the neckline, a flare at the lower hem, and silver stars woven into the fabric. The feeling of the scene is of the old-time movies of black and white, where the dames and gents dress formally all day.

We greet each other. This princess shows me she has a pea. A pea like you might have on your dinner plate tonight. And I'm being reminded that yes, she could do many things with it. Drop it, plant it, squish it, give it away, throw it away—many things! She swaps the pea to her other hand and holds it for a moment as she keeps her focus on me. The pea suddenly pops like a kernel of corn would pop in a pot that is hot. And she pops it in her mouth and swallows it down. She winks at me as if to say, "You didn't expect that, did you?" without saying a word.

Well, no. No, I did not.

She turns to resume walking along the forest trail we are both on. She invites me to join her as we walk to the castle ahead. She says, "You didn't expect me to be walking in the mud and the muck here on this trail, did you, in this fine, fine dress, with my fine, fine shoes?"

"No, I did not expect that," I say good-heartedly, well aware my own shoes are getting soiled with each step I take.

She talks of her day as we walk along some more. We finally arrive at the castle, and we are welcomed inside. Her father, the king of the fair land, is on the throne in the throne room, and he is doing kingly things, and he is wearing kingly clothes, and there are courtiers around as we walk into the lavishly appointed room.

He greets her warmly and asks for her opinion on certain subjects that have come up that day. She gives her strategies freely. The king makes decrees based on what she says. She turns to me and says in a voice only I can hear, "You didn't expect that, did you?" We take our leave of the court and go into the dining room for a meal.

The queen is there in the dining hall, and some staff are attending there too. Some visiting dignitaries are there as well. There's much fussing, in a formal way. Many say hello to the fair princess and inquire about her day.

Names are easily remembered, and backstories told, and conversations continue from where they were left off months ago. People move to clear a way for the princess and I to proceed to the head of the table. She looks at the food in front of her and informs the staff to take it away. It is not good enough.

"Give us the best. Give us the freshest. This bread is day old, and this meat looks like it needs to be fed to the dogs." Right away the princess turns to me and says, "You didn't expect that, did you?" The princess continues, "You thought maybe I would just go along with it. You thought maybe I would just play along and eat this slop?"

She motions for me to follow her as she exits the dining hall. She and I climb the staircase together. We arrive at her suite's door. She smiles and holds up her hand as she quietly slips inside, alone.

I wait outside in the grand hall, alone.

She emerges in tomboy clothes more suitable for play, suitable for getting dirty in the muck. She has her hair tied back now, and she exclaims, "Let's play!" She runs down the long hall to the servant staircase as I rush to keep up. She bounces down the stairs and then dashes through more halls to get outside. As soon as we are outside the walls, she rolls on the grass, and she enjoys the day, and she squeals, and she's laughing at the joy of it all. She picks up a little bit of mud and throws it my way. I pick up a little bit too and gently throw it back at her. She easily dodges, and she wipes her hands on her pants. She puts a little dirt on her nose while pretending to ignore me.

She says, "You didn't expect that, did you?"

No, I did not expect a grown princess to roll on the ground. Or to take such delight at the simple things.

She motions with a hooked thumb and a nod of her head towards the horse stables. I notice a gleam in her eye before she turns to fast walk there. She picks the finest steed, the tallest one, the strongest one. She jumps on its bare back, and puts her heels into his flank, and away they go! I grab the nearest horse to give chase. Soon they are out of sight in the forest heavy with trees, even as I ride this old mare hard after her, but I can follow her laughter and I know where we are riding to. Up the mountain, up the mountain, there's a trail, there's a trail!

Finally, I catch up to her. She has already stopped by a stream. It's her favourite spot in the sun. "You didn't expect that," is all she says as she jumps down from her mighty horse.

"You expected me to have footmen, and horsemen, and soldiers around, but no. Not here. I go out by myself sometimes and enjoy nature. This isn't my bathing spot, but you're not ready to see that yet. This is my enjoyment spot." She asks if I want refreshments.

I simply reply, "Yes."

She looks around and she realizes with a smile there are simply no refreshments to be had. No one to serve, no one to cater. Simply her and me, and two horses by a stream. She reaches down into the water, scoops up some water for herself, and brings what water she can hold in her hands to the steed. I take the hint and also scoop water for myself and my horse, who refuses the drink.

The princess raises her horse's hooves one by one and tends to fixing one of the horseshoes that is loose. She jumps on her horse and tests the horseshoe fix. Satisfied, she says to me, "You didn't expect that."

No, I did not expect that.

She races down the hill towards the castle, her blond hair flowing in the wind as her horse gallops strong and fast with his hooves now properly shod. I push my trusty mare, but she is winded now and can't keep up to the younger horse. I hear laughter as the girl disappears on the trail.

I catch sight of her again, as I come out of the forest near the village. She spurs her trotting steed to match my mare's speed. The sentry soldiers make way for us as we gallop through the gates. We come to the stables, and she hands her steed off to a stable boy. I turn my back for a moment, and somehow she has changed into clothing most dire. A hood for her head to cloak who she is. Her new outfit is already dirty. Her clothes are quite common, even more than before.

She nods at me saying, "Let's get that refreshment. Let's go to the pub!"

Aghast, I look at her as my jaw drops. A princess in a pub?

She cajoles, "Come on!" Into the smoke, into the grime, into where the common folk go. She sits down at the bar, nods to the barman, and two drinks appear. She knocks one back and as I reach for mine, she grabs my drink and knocks it back as well.

She laughs as she throws some coins on the bar. She shouts, "Two more!" to the barman and offers me one when they arrive. "You didn't expect that."

No, I did not.

She motions with her arm to the crowd quite noisy. "These are our friends here. You will see."

She gets up on the stage. Someone has a lute and gets up to play it. The princess starts singing. The crowd pays attention. Conversations go quiet. She sings a song of love. She sings a song of beauty. She sings a song of heartache far beyond her years. She finishes her last tune, all most beautifully sung.

Applause. Someone throws a flower at her feet. She smiles and walks off stage.

"You didn't expect that, did you?"

No, I did not.

"Come, let's go to the castle's inner chamber. You'll know the one."

Her cloak now tossed aside, we walk directly into the keep's war room—there are strong men and pudgy men, and maps with little figures in formation, and weapons on the wall. Her father is there in discussion with his advisors. They go quiet as she approaches. She surveys the war map and she understands the stage.

She says this, she says that. She says this, she says that, and the men agree to a man that "detente" will be the word of the day.

She looks at me fully and casually brushes some dirt off my shoulder I hadn't noticed before. "You didn't expect that, did you?"

No, I did not.

We stroll out of the room. She motions for me to come sit on a bench in a now-quiet hallway. "There were many things today that you did not expect," she states.

"Yes, that is quite right."

"Why do you judge? Why do you feel that way? Why do you think the way you do? Cannot this form, this giggly girl, do this, do that, and do this other thing too?"

"Well, um. Yes. I mean, of course! I—"

"What!?"

"I just didn't expect it in one package."

"That's because I listened to my heart, and I listened to yours. We can be friends for now. Kiss me and let's start again."

The Change

She is in a record store. A 1980's era record store, with big promotional posters hanging from the ceiling featuring the likes of Madonna and Bon Jovi. One of the overhead florescent lights is burned out, and there is an electrical hum. There are many album jackets featuring big hair and leather on the covers. The girl is in her early 20s, and she is wearing a leather miniskirt, fishnet stockings, and a few pieces of costume jewelry. She is skirting with being called "goth light" by prudish strangers, but she enjoys the look. She likes how she looks. She likes how she feels inside wearing these clothes on the outside. But she hasn't gone all in with her fashion—her hair is a natural chestnut brown with a slight natural wave and it is shoulder length. Some may judge her harshly on her choices, but she knows who she is, and she walks with a confident air.

I get the feeling she was just about ready to throw a record at me last time I looked her way, so let's just sneak a peek at what she is doing now...

She's made her selection. It's a rock and roll record. The music is not as soft as I thought it might be, nor is it as hard as I feared it might be. She goes up to pay at the counter, and she very meticulously lays the record down on the counter for the clerk.

She and the clerk exchange polite conversation, for they know each other a little bit, as she has been into the store before. She opens up her purse and very properly pulls out bills that are folded. The bills are folded in four. She hands the proper bills over, getting the change back. She keeps the paper, and she puts the silver onto the counter for the clerk to put towards concert tickets. She folds, she meticulously folds, the paper money, closes up her purse, takes her purchase bag, and says thank you to her friend the clerk.

We next catch up with her outside the store a block or so away. She's enjoying the day. Her beautiful young skin is just glowing in the springtime sunshine. Her subdued yet also stark makeup looks great on her alabaster skin. As I said, she is enjoying the day. I am sure in her mind, she's thinking she's walking along to one of the tunes from a Doris Day movie. A tune that is super happy, with a kind of bubble gum feel, which again isn't quite in line with what the girl has got going on in terms of her fashion. But she's happy inside. And the world can see that. The world can feel that she is joyous.

One of her friends waves from across the street and approaches her at the corner when the crosswalk light approves. She excitedly blabs to the friend the good news she just got—she was promoted at work and she bought a record to celebrate! She's making some extra money, you know, and life is good. The friends hug and part after another moment of talking. She goes into the park. There is a city park nearby here, and it is a beautiful day for a stroll after a long winter of grey clouds.

There are families out. There are dogs and frisbees and, you know, all kinds of the stuff that goes on in cities that are alive and vibrant with citizens that are engaged in life in all its glory. She goes up to one of the food vendors, a hot dog vendor, and says, "I'll take your best smokie."

She again meticulously pulls out her meticulously folded paper money and hands it to the man, who by appearance is of Italian descent and weighs upwards of 250 pounds. And again, there is silver change coming back to her from her payment, and she directs him to put it into the tip jar that's there. It's a clear tip jar, and she can see it needs a little boost. A little bit there in the jar goes a long way with this working man's family.

She strolls over a ways away from the food cart area and sits on a bench. She's, you know, sitting quite properly with her purse on her lap as she is watching the dogs play, and watching the kiddos play, and aware that the parents are in small groups, talking up a storm. She is just waiting for her smokie to be cooked.

"Okay. Okay. Miss, yours is ready now!" The hot dog vendor calls her over after a few short minutes with a wave. Yes, her turn is up for a lunch delight!

She goes to the cart to collect her lunch and apply some of the good stuff to it. I'm seeing jalapeños, some mustard, and just a little bit of ketchup go onto her smokie bun. She grabs a few napkins before setting off for a walk 'n eat.

She is walking along in the busy park… and oh no! She's not quite noticing what is going on around her. She is not paying as much attention to where she is walking as she maybe should. She bumps into a young businessman who may be in his late 20s. He is quite well dressed, quite well. You know the type with his fresh haircut and nice suit. She gets the tiniest amount of mustard on his lapel. And it's a very, very small amount. But, of course, she's horrified, for that is who she is. She offers to have it dry cleaned and she has napkins, of course, to share in the meantime.

And, of course, he doesn't quite know what to make of this girl dressed in black, but it is a minor incident, and he is on his way elsewhere. He informs her he has it from here. She kind of blushes a little bit at her mistake and his harsh rebuke. She moves off, and he moves off, continuing to rush wherever he was going.

There is a moment where they get 10 paces from each other and then they both stop cold and pause. They turn around to walk towards the other. Some might say they rushed towards each other in that moment. And they say hello at the same time. She starts saying, "I am so sorry." He starts saying, "Hey, it's okay, you know, it's okay, but who are you? Who are you? Who are you to me? You have a beautiful smile, and I was just going to have lunch by myself at a restaurant I know. Let me buy you lunch, to replace the hot dog I ruined."

A stunned look crosses her face before she regains control of her reaction, and she pauses to think for a moment because she still has a perfectly good smokie in her hand. The little angel on her shoulder, the good angel, is saying, "Go, go for lunch. Go, go for lunch." And she says to the businessman, "Sure. I will go for lunch. But so you know, it was a smokie I was eating, not a hot dog."

His name is Josh. Her name is Angela. They walk for a little bit, and it turns out it is not far to the restaurant he had in mind. It's a beautiful restaurant, one of those beautiful eateries with a breath-taking view of the city's beautiful working harbour.

They know him there. "Come right this way! Your usual table is available, sir," and, of course, he has been there a hundred times, and he knows who the staff are by name, though he never thought to ask about their home lives. Angela hasn't been there before, and she's looking around, her eyes wide, kind of like Julia Roberts in one of her movies when she is starstruck. They sit down.

It's a beautiful view with boats and planes and freighters in the distance. Water and bread are brought to the table, and all that usual stuff, with a little bit of chitchat with the staff. Angela meticulously puts her own napkin on her own lap and sits properly. Josh sits very casually, more like he's in a pub with his college buddies—he has one arm over the spare chair and one arm resting on the table. He is looking at the scenery, but his mind is elsewhere. For he is thinking about somehow starting the conversation off right. He ponders asking the usual first-date type stuff, except it is not a date. It can't be a date.

"What do you do?" he decides to say. "Where do you live? And what is going on in your world?"

She answers him, meticulously and properly. She shares enough to be polite and keep the conversation going but does not overly share. And his three questions are answered, and then she, of course, says, "What do you do, sir?"

Turns out that he is a criminal lawyer. He defends the bad guys. He defends the actual guilty parties. And he's getting sick of that but he decides there is no way he is telling her that. So he settles for telling her he wants to do more in life by helping the good guys win cases instead of helping the bad guys get away with murder, so to speak, literally. Then, for some reason, he starts telling her a short version of his life story. He winds up confiding he is okay with a pay cut to be a prosecuting attorney, but it's the prestige of his current position in private practice that he would miss, and he doesn't know how to proceed exactly. There are family issues. Expectations put on him by his parents to do this, that, and the other thing. The right things. There is also a long-term girlfriend who is in the picture of his life. He reminds himself that this strange woman is out of the picture—this lunch is just paying her back for her lunch he ruined by running into her at the park. His girlfriend and his parents are pushing for marriage, and his own "shoulder angels" have been saying for many weeks now, "Wait, wait, wait, wait, wait." He is still not sure why he is telling this girl how his life resembles a meat grinder, although he realizes he is comfortable around her.

She thinks to her own wallet, which is not as full as it could be, but it is meticulously folded and planned. She thinks for a moment and then looks him square in the eyes. She relays to him that money is wonderful, prestige is wonderful, but happiness is important too. "I've never been to this restaurant. It is beautiful, but I was happy before I came to this place, and I will be happy when I leave this restaurant after a nice meal and a nice conversation with you. Josh, don't you see, you are going to be in turmoil for a day, or two, or five or more, from when we leave this restaurant. What would make you happy?" she asks as a softness creeps into her eyes.

There is silence between them for a long moment, and he looks away from her. He says, "I am not close friends with anyone in the DA's office, but I can certainly make some phone calls."

She kind of smiles and blushes a little as she flicks her hair out of her eyes. She says, "No. No. Go knock on doors and go see the people there in person. Don't you have some sick time coming or holiday time to use up?"

He starts to smirk like a little boy at her suggestion and he goes, "Yeah, actually, I do. I can actually take this afternoon off, in fact."

"Well, go do that."

The meal arrives, and it's beautiful. The two new friends talk about everything under the sun, but they don't go back to the serious topic. They keep it light. The bill comes.

The bill is paid. They walk each other out, and she starts to walk away.

He calls to her and says, "Well, hey! What do you have going on this afternoon? Do you want to come to the public defender's office with me?"

She says she will walk part of the way, but he needs to open that particular door on his own. So they walk. He reaches for her hand. They walk, and they talk some more, and they giggle a little bit too. Another secret, or two, shared, and he says softly, "You don't fit into my world. You are not like anybody else I've ever met. None of my friends wear black lipstick."

She smiles that knowing smile of hers and says, "Yeah, well, I know fashion. I know what's proper."

They walk for another moment or two until she says, "This is my turn. I live down this street. See you later."

"Can I see you again?" he says before she goes.

"No! No. Get the job, and if you get the job that you want and you break up with the girl and you tell your parents to go stuff themselves, then come look for me. I'll be down by the docks. I'm usually there around seven every night enjoying the sunset. Bring me a smokie. Maybe some ice cream. I'll be there." She walks away without looking back.

He watches her go. The way she walks, and the way people smile as they pass her, he can tell she's happy. She's living life on her own terms. Part of him imagines her living in a small, cramped apartment, with barely enough room to turn around, while he is going to go back to a very large home. And he wonders if he'll ever be happy in that large empty home.

He sets off for the public defender's office. It goes well.

Later, as his stomach growls, he finally remembers he set up a dinner date for later that same night with his girlfriend. They haven't spoken, really spoken, that is, for a while now. They meet for dinner, and he kisses her on the cheek. They sit and chat, but there's a certain strained quality to the conversation. A certain something's shifted, for something has changed inside him. His mind drifts to proposing they take a break from the relationship while she talks of her day and the horrible people she met.

Then something kind of snaps, something inside of him snaps, and he abruptly says, "No, I want to break up. This isn't working for me the way it's going. And you're not really the person for me. Marriage would be a mistake."

The girlfriend's face turns ashen. She didn't expect that outburst. There's a bit of a scene between the two of them, with everyone in the restaurant staring at her as she goes on her way.

The maître d' from lunchtime is still working. He comes over to the table and remarks, "Oh, you don't look happy, sir. You looked happier at lunch."

"Yes. Yes, I did. I have some phone calls to make. Here. Keep the change."

The Shipwreck

I have dropped into the water. It is cold. I am not supposed to be in the water. I am concerned. My ears are ringing, my vision is wonky, and I am confused about what is happening.

I thrash around, completely covered by bubbles and cold water spray. I am a little scared. This is not normal. I am holding my breath. I breach the water after a moment and begin treading water.

I hear screams and yelling through my waterlogged ears. I see a broken ship in the distance. I feel the waves slapping my head. I see a wood plank close by, so I swim towards it and grab it. At least now I can float. Thoughts rampage through my frantic mind, "Where is my family? Where are my friends? Where are the people who were just at the dinner table? Where is the captain?"

Oh no, I can see dead bodies. I can see dead bodies that are floating in the rough seas.

There is a storm approaching. There are lightning flashes in the distance. It may rain at any moment. I don't know what happened earlier, but I am scared and alone, and there is no one around. I have the plank, though, and I hang on for dear life. I am okay at the moment. I close my eyes to clear the tears from the water spray, then look down at my body. I am wearing a sailor suit. It had been very starched. It had been very white. Maybe I am part of the crew of the ship that is broken and torn?

Where are my buddies? Are they okay? I look around and I finally see someone I know in the distance. I swim towards him. He has no hat on. He always has a hat on. He is spitting water and he is not doing well. He is talking about a wound on his leg. I go towards him as best I can, the waves slapping me, making progress difficult. I get to him and I offer him an edge of the board. It sinks a little bit. Just a little bit. I don't think we could have another man share the board now, weighing it down.

I look around again and this time spot a dark-haired man. I call him over. He grabs onto the plank, and it sinks even more with his added weight. He seems to have a wound on his back of some sort. He is complaining about his back anyway. It is a little hard to hear him above all the other noise. I realize I am doing better than my friends. I am not injured. I am just dazed.

I let go of the board. It rises up just a little bit. The two of them are okay to hang on, and I can tread water for a bit. There is more debris coming into view. There is more wood. There are more planks. There are more survivors. Thank God.

Oh, a wave reveals a dead body I hadn't noticed before. He is face down. I don't want to see who it is. I might know him.

There are buckets in the debris. Pillows, and bedding too. Things that can float.

Where is help? There must be help! The ship is burning, so there is light for help to see us. Where is help?

More of the survivors gather nearby. The waves are not quite as wild as they were a moment ago. We can see each other and we call out. We know to dog paddle towards each other. I see a lifeboat in the distance. The group of men in the lifeboat are picking up people as fast as they can. There is another lifeboat even further away, so some of us will make it.

Where is help? There should be help!

Lightning flashes in the distance, closer this time. The flash of the lightning bolt brings a ship into view against the dark horizon.

My heart goes dark. It is the enemy's ship. It is the one that sank us.

They are moving away. They will not finish what they started. I suppose they think we are just not worth looking for.

I look around, and maybe half the crew survived. The lifeboats are saving as many as possible. The boats are overcrowded already, and we are very far out from even the closest lifeboat—me, the first buddy, and the dark-haired buddy, and the little plank. The rescuers haven't noticed us quite yet.

I try to help the other men by telling them to be strong, be positive, and hang on to the plank. My dark-haired friend talks about his wife and his kids. Our blonde friend tells him to shut up, for he is single still, but I know there is a girl he is fond of—a girl he writes to. He hadn't had a chance to let her know how he felt. How he really felt about her. Now he might never get the chance to. You ever seen a grown man cry? Well… yeah…

One of the lifeboats finally does see us. They paddle our way with their oars straining but they are full. There is no room. We hang onto the side of the boat. Other men hang onto some rope that is tied to the lifeboat. Someone volunteers to give up his seat for my buddy with the sore leg. We struggled to get him in the boat, but now he has a seat. He can rest. He doesn't move too well. Nobody is really moving well.

There are more bodies. More debris floats by us. One more explosion rattles us all before our ship sinks out of sight for good.

I hang onto the side of the lifeboat that rescued us an hour or so ago. I hear the men talk amongst themselves. Someone is freaking out, and someone tries to console him. The lifeboats have come mostly together. That's what you do when there is tragedy. You move together in companionship. Someone curses and throws his wet cigarettes overboard in disgust; they are wet and they ain't gonna light.

The other ship has moved off now, nowhere in sight. Off for another kill.

The storm holds off for now. There is someone in charge now. Someone who knows. He says they will come looking for us, our friends. They know where we are, more or less. The battle fleet will come looking.

I ask him, "How long?"

He blusters and says, "Not long."

I don't take the hint and ask him again, "How long?"

"Three days. Three days at maximum speed."

"Oh uh." Three days. The men fall into despair and go quiet. It starts to rain. The rain comes down hard as the heavens open up. Misery upon misery.

Dawn breaks on a new day, and there is no land in sight. I rub the sleep from my eyes and slowly remember our ship has sunk and her debris is scattered. We get our bearings and slowly row towards where we think help might come from. We row half-heartedly. There is no water, no food. Someone has a soggy chocolate bar. He shares it, but it is not enough. The lifeboats have some food in cans that tastes like shoe leather. It is food, though—something to share, something to talk about, something to complain about.

Day fades into dark. We huddle to keep warm. We take turns being overboard, those who can, and those who will. It is not strange to hug another man for warmth when you are freezing cold and hungry.

My best buddy is in the next lifeboat. I know he is alive. It is good to have confirmation.

Night turns into day, and day turns into night. Things are bleak—men have died in the boats, so we throw them overboard to make room for the living. Feels very strange to do that, but what else can we do?

Daylight rolls around again, bright as can be. Stomachs are empty, and throats are parched. Pants are soiled. Another man dies, and I hear groaning.

Then someone yells, "Smoke on the horizon. They have found us!" There is hope!

Those who can look to see. Yes, there is smoke. Could be a ship! Could even be several ships, but are they friend or foe? Do we care?

Someone gets overly excited and stands up for a better look, rocking the lifeboat he is in. He gets hauled down. Don't rock the boat. Be steady and calm. Hold on. The day goes on, and the smoke comes closer. Stan, the eagle-eyed cook confirms our best hopes, "Yes, it is our friends!" The men get happier. There is joy. There is hope.

The ship comes closer and closer. Even the men with vacant eyes start to rejoice and wave. Some of the men jump in the water and swim towards the friendly ship. Seems strange they would do that when the ship is far away from us.

The steam ship finally comes alongside, having seen us. It is ours. Our friends. The ship is small, though—almost too small—but then, we are a small group. The men on board jump down, giving ropes and ladders and help to those who are struggling. We do our best to take care of the injured men and get them up to safety.

It is a hospital ship! It is already full to the rafters, but there is help for our injured. It is not from our battlegroup. The ship is on a mission, a mission to go home.

Home.

Home sounds nice.

There is no room for our lifeboats. We cast them adrift, for we are all safe and sound on a hospital ship.

The Baker

The scene is late evening in a small bakery. There is a baker getting things ready for a big bake day tomorrow. He is doing this and doing that to get ready. He has flour and sugar all over himself from a hard day's work of prepping, and baking, and serving customers, and getting things just right for the big day, though he works this hard every day, really. He's a little bit older than he feels he is, you know, perhaps in his 50s, perhaps in his 60s. He still has dark hair and a dark moustache.

He is a hefty man from enjoying his own products — which are very, very good! People come from miles around to purchase his baked goods. His family has been baking for generation upon generation, and he has many "secret recipes" floating around in his head. This isn't the original location of the family bakery, but it is certainly a well-loved and well-used replacement bakery that conveniently has a house attached to it.

He is getting ready for a wedding tomorrow and he wants to make sure that the ingredients for the breads and the buns and all of the sweet things that he will make are in place and just perfect. Everything needs to be perfect, for the bride is a much-loved local girl who worked at the bakery for a few summers when she was younger. His wife comes in and, knowing him as she does, she scolds him a little bit about how "his dinner was served hours ago and is now cold and he needs to get to bed because he's going to be up early tomorrow."

And he says lovingly to her, "Yes, yes, you're right. I need to do a few more little things and then I'll be there."

He gets the last of the dried apricots ready. He gets some chocolate ready for tomorrow. He doesn't wish to rush tomorrow.

Finally, everything's ready. Organized. He looks back at the bakery as he starts to leave. He breathes in, and he thinks of his papa and his papa before him and his papa before him and how it feels good to bake and see the smiles on people's faces. It feels good to be of service, and he is glad that his neighbours are able to enjoy his wonderful breads and treats. He turns the lights off, closes the door, and goes into the house. Momma is there and she scolds him again, "Well, dear husband, your dinner is cold, but here's the plate. Come sit down."

And he sits down at the table, with his glass of wine, the good food, and she now wants to reheat it all over again. And he says, "No, Momma. Cold is good. Cold is good," as he gently reaches with his loving hand to take hers reaching for his plate to reheat his dinner.

He tells of his day, and she tells of her day. The dinner plate becomes empty. The wine is touched, but it is not finished. Not with an early day tomorrow. She gets up to clear the dinner table. She had already eaten when the food was hot from the oven, as she has learned to do. He moves towards her, and gently takes the empty plate from her hands, and puts the plate down again.

She looks at him quizzically. He puts an arm around her waist, and then a hand in a hand, and he starts to dance, and he starts to hum, and he starts to sing, and he starts to move like they did when they were younger.

"Oh," as she rolls her eyes. "Oh. Oh, you handsome man!" She teases him but she is very loving, very kind while saying it. And they swing around a little bit in the dining room, and she says something about needing to do the dishes, needing to clean up.

"Oh, leave that for tomorrow. Tonight we'll be young and tonight we will dance!"

And she kind of giggles at his outburst of playfulness and softens into him and puts her head on his shoulder. And they dance for a moment longer, and then he leans in to kiss her with a passion still strong even after all these years and tears.

He says, "Momma, leave the dishes. Let's just go to bed!" And he picks her up in his strong arms and carries her into the bedroom. He flips the door closed with his foot.

The next morning, the rooster starts crowing. The sun is up. It's time to work.

Our baker friend gets up and looks at his wife, who is still sleeping in bed. He smiles and gets ready for the workday. He goes into the bakery, and the next thing Momma hears is a scream. She rushes downstairs in her night coat and says, "What is wrong, honey? What is wrong?"

"Ah, there are tracks. Look, it's ruined. Look, the little footprints have tracked flour all over my counter that was clean last night!"

Momma looks. Momma's quite concerned that he could be so upset on this big day. She comes over and looks at the counter he pointed to. He's already off in the storeroom, searching through the bags of fruit and sacks of flour and sugar. Though there is still sleep in her eyes, she looks over to the counter and sees the footprints. But they do not look like mouse tracks. And she calls to him and says, "Honey, I'm not sure it's a mouse. They have different feet, don't they?"

"Oh, it's a mouse. It's a mouse! It's a mouse!" He starts tearing apart the storeroom. He wants to make sure there are no droppings or ripped bags, and you know, if there are 10 bags in the storeroom, there are a hundred bags! His mind races as he considers how many people would be disappointed in him if there were in fact a mouse in his bakery. His ability to provide for his family is on the line. His neighbours, if they found out there was a mouse, what would they do? Would they still come and shop and eat his good bread? He pauses his search to ponder if they would stay away for good … his father and his father before him would be turning over in their graves … his family's safety is on the line.

"No, Momma. No, Momma," he mutters as he starts looking through the bags again and making quite a mess of the now messy storeroom, disorganizing it by moving everything around haphazardly and spilling some ingredients on the floor.

Momma opens and closes her eyes a few times, trying to wake up and think clearly about the situation. She looks around the main area. There are no mouse droppings, there are no holes, there is nothing untoward. There is no sign of a mouse. There is no sign of an intruder.

She looks in the bags of ingredients that are out front. She looks in the sacks in the storeroom. She looks in the … everywhere … that she could possibly look, and there is still no sign of a mouse! She can hear the baker banging around in the back of the storeroom, and she calls again to him, "Honey, honey! I'm not sure it was a mouse at all! There is no sign of it. There are no droppings. There are no more foot tracks. There is no ... there is no flour spilled for the mouse to track! You had it all sealed up! And wouldn't there be mouse tracks in the supply room coming to the counter if there was a mouse?"

He slows down, but he doesn't stop. He turns to look directly at her, and he considers what she's saying, realization slowly coming to him. He sees her as the way she is now in the early morning light with her face filled with worry, but as he continues to gaze and ponder, he plainly sees that she starts to glow very slightly, as if her skin was shiny. In that moment, he also sees her as the way she was sleeping peacefully this morning, and he also sees her as she looked sleeping at first light of the morning after their wedding, all those fine years ago. He shakes his head and blinks his eyes before continuing as if nothing happened, "But the tracks! What are the tracks? There is a mess on the counter, and I was, I was cleaning last night and I made sure—"

"I don't know, sweetheart, but you come and look. Come and look. Leave what you're doing husband. Come and look here with me."

He comes to the front area, and he now sees that indeed she is right. There are no obvious mouse signs. There are no obvious droppings.

There is nothing out of place except for a little bit of flour on the counter. And it is in a peculiar shape. As his wife looks around in the calm, cold light, she spies a spoon on the floor that had been washed and was hanging to dry by the sink. When she brings it over and she puts it over top of the counter to the flour track, it fits perfectly! "It looks like this is our culprit. It's a spoon that hit this open bowl of flour, and you might not have—"

"Just stop there," he says. "I cleaned everything. I made sure! You know that's what we do!"

"Yes, Papa, but it doesn't look like a mouse print and it's got ... Here is the spoon. Maybe you were too tired. Maybe you just missed it. Maybe it was dark. Did you have your glasses on? You missed lunch and you had a late dinner. There are many things that could have happened, honey."

He looks at her. He starts to see her wisdom through the love in her eyes. The visions of her he had just moments ago come back strongly, aiding to melt his stubborn concern. His brain can't quite fathom that he made a mistake of that nature, that he missed something. It's still early, and neither of them have had tea or breakfast. She puts the spoon in the sink, and says, "Come on, Papa. Let me make you some tea. We'll get some breakfast into you, and then you can start working." His mind is still reeling, but he agrees to have breakfast. They close the door to the bakery and go into the house.

She makes some tea. She puts together some breakfast—hot this time with eggs and some of the bacon that he loves, and, of course, some bread and some sweets from his bakery. His mind starts to calm down. She hums a little bit of a tune and touches him on his arm. She prattles on, distracting him with small talk and prodding him with questions that have nothing to do with baking. She knows him. She knows him, and he knows her.

There's a beautiful moment of connection between them, and he snaps out of the rage, and the worry, and the overthinking, the overanalyzing. "Maybe I did miss something, Momma. Maybe I did. I have been working hard lately. There's so much to do with this wedding. It's very important—"

"It's beautiful what you are preparing. You are doing great work, honey. The cake is amazing. But maybe after this ... Let's go away for a few days. My sister lives an easy day's travel from here, and she's been asking us to visit for a while now. The blossoms are out, and you know how much I love seeing them. It would be a beautiful time to go visit her."

"Perhaps you're right. Perhaps you're right." He finishes his breakfast.

She finishes her breakfast, too, and pours another cup of tea for both of them. He gets up and kisses her gently on the cheek. He goes to the bakery and does what he needs to do that morning. He chooses to leave the supply room as is for now, but he makes the buns, and the bread, and the treats, right and fresh. The day goes on, and everything comes out of the oven hot and fresh, as planned.

People come and pick up baking for the wedding. They not only pay for it but leave a good tip. "Thank you, and I remind you, good sir, that you are invited to the wedding too." Momma and Papa will be there. They know everyone, and everyone knows them.

The evening comes. The bakery couple have dressed up in their finest. They go to the wedding, and it's a beautiful ceremony. People say greetings as they pass by, and others stop to say hello and inquire how they are. The long workdays this week, and this morning's harrowing event are long forgotten by both of them. The reception is a feast—the beautiful food, the venison roast, the root vegetables, the baking, and the treats on the sweet table. Such a beautiful wedding, and such a beautiful reception!

The bride is glowing. Papa, the baker, feels so proud that his baking is there at the center plate on the center table. The meal is finished, and the bride and groom start on their rounds to thank everyone. They approach the bakery couple. "The treats were delicious," the bride gushes.

"The bread was delicious, and that cake was just divine!" agrees the groom.

Papa looks at Momma. He gently squeezes her hand and says to the couple, "We are going away for a day or two—maybe a little more, to see her family and enjoy the countryside. You two are just starting out. We wish you much happiness, just as we've been happy together all these years we've been married." His gaze lingers on his wife for a sweet moment longer and then turns again to face the newlyweds. "Bride, you worked for me a few summers ago. I'm wondering, when you're ready, if you'd like to come back and spend some time in the bakery—both of you! Both of you come! We can teach ... maybe, maybe you two would want to take it over one day..."

He blinks a tear away, clears his throat that got suddenly thick, and continues as the three adults take in what Papa is asking. "Groom, we have no children, but I look at Momma the way you look at your bride. Think about it. Go on your honeymoon, and when you come back, we can talk."

Life begins anew and life keeps going like the bread that rises. Sometimes it just needs to be kneaded.

The Girl

I have entered a dimly lit large room. There is a little girl just sitting in this room all alone. Petite. She might remind you of a cartoony kind of character in a manner of speaking—she has big, big eyes with curly, dirty blonde hair. She is wearing a green and white sundress, in a style suitable and cute for a little girl who looks like she may be four years old.

She looks sad to me as she sits there at a pint-size table all alone. She stares with vacant eyes looking at the floor. I'm seeing a lot of unwashed white pine as I scan around the room. The room is kind of dark, in a kind of not-lit-very-well way. There is a bit of a spotlight halfheartedly shining on her table, and by extension herself, and her hair, which glows a little in the soft, pale light.

I come up to her, and she is not crying, exactly. She is not talkative, exactly. She is not exactly responding at all. I clear my throat and ask her if it is okay to sit down at the empty chair next to her. She doesn't exactly say yes, but she doesn't exactly say no either. She kind of shrugs—at least I think it is a shrug—so I take a chance that means I can sit down here. I sit down. As you can imagine, it's a little comical that the adult I am, a fully grown adult, is sitting on a child-size chair. I noticed the humour. It's a little ... not quite right.

She notices it too. She looks out of the corner of her eyes as if asking, "And who are you?"

I think about how to get the conversation started, and so I comment about the room being kind of dark, and how the girl doesn't have anything in front of her. There are no stuffies, games, or cards, or paints, or cell phones, or really anything to be seen that a little girl might like around on her table.

She starts by talking about writing. She is talking about actual pen-and-paper-type writing that she wants to do. She looks at me with those big eyes, not quite as vacant looking as they were when I glimpsed them a moment ago. I see her eyes are a shade of green, with a few blue specks in them. They've got gorgeous, absolutely gorgeous black pupils, real inky black pupils. I get the strong feeling she is sad. You might remember I said that already. She stops my reverie cold as she asks, "Are you sad?" instead.

I'm taken aback by that question. I thought I was here to rescue her from this lonesome room. I sit up to look around like an adult does when startled, scanning the room in a more logical way than I did a moment ago, and I say, "Well, yeah. This room has a kind of sadness about it that seeps into one's bones. You know, it makes me sad just being in this room. There is not much light. There is a little girl here with not much to do, all by her lonesome.

And frankly, this chair is killing me. My sciatica is flaring up."

"Oh," is what she says before her eyes lose what little glow they had, becoming sad once more. She looks away, her vacant gaze returning to the floor.

She looks back at me after a moment and she continues, "But you don't have to be here!"

I am flabbergasted again at the turn of conversation with this child.

She lets me know that, "You can do whatever you want. You don't have to be in this room!" I look back at her from looking around the room again to make sure I am the one she is talking to. Her eyes once more have a glow to them.

"Well, you are right, but I was drawn here because of you."

"Oh. Well, that's peculiar," is what she says. "I haven't seen anyone for a long, long time. Bathroom is over there," she says as she points. "There are just cookies left on the counter. The milk in the fridge went sour, but there is some juice. You can have some if you want. I can share," she confides quietly to me as her focus moves off to stare at the floor again.

I go to stand up, but I'm sitting at such a low angle that standing is difficult for me. I fall down on one knee. The damn low chair is awkward. The table is awkward. The room is awkward, and I am awkward in this dull, dim, dark room with a strange girl I don't know or recognize.

She gets up. She comes over. She doesn't help me get up but she looks long and hard at me and finally says, "I know you."

I decide to swing my legs so I can sit on the floor cross-legged, trying to get back some of my dignity that I might have lost when I fell.

She comes over to sit in my lap like little children do when they are comfortable, when they trust someone. She starts telling me a tale of dragons, and knights in armour, and claws, and fire. Stories of knights that were burned, stories of women that were abducted, stories of villages that were destroyed. She gets up from where she was sitting, and she grabs my face with both her little hands. She pulls my eyes down to her level and asks, "Who was the bad guy? Who was the victor?" After a pause, "Do you know?"

I state, "I don't know."

She waves her arms about and bursts out, "Nobody! Nobody was the victor! Men died. Women died. Villages were burned. Dragons died. The wounded went home and were never the same. No one was the winner! No one was the victor! Hearts became hard! Walls were built! Laws enacted!

"This fighting didn't last very long. It couldn't. It was too fierce." She sees puzzlement and horror raging across my face, and she continues in a softer voice, "Well yes, the fighting eventually stopped, but something worse happened." She pauses again and tilts her head up to look into my face.

"Do you know what happened next?" she asks with an even softer voice than before.

"No, I don't." I say gently. "Please tell me," as I start to stealthily stretch a little bit to get comfortable here on the hard floor. I wonder if the table would hold my weight if I sat on it.

"Humans forgot! Humans forgot how to be kind, how to talk, how to live with one another." She raises her hand for emphasis. "They killed, they raped, they burned, they slaughtered. Not that their enemies were any better. There was blood on all hands! All claws! There were many children that grew up that year whether they were ready to or not." She crosses her arms as she looks away from me yet again.

It is my turn to pause and reflect. I make a connection in my mind and I ask her if that's when she came here to this room.

"A little while after that," she says as she returns her gaze to me. "Let me finish my story."

"Please do," is what I say.

The girl snuggles back into my lap and continues, "The humans, they forgot about the dragons. Slowly, over time, they forgot. They rebuilt their villages, then they built small cities, then they built bigger cities. They made weapons, and then they made bigger weapons. There were no dragons left to kill, so the humans killed each other. For even the slightest little reason, they would go to war with their neighbours. Sometimes if you walk quietly in certain places, you can still hear the soldiers' screams from long ago."

She shifts her body to look up at me to make sure I'm still listening. Her big, colourful eyes glow as if reacting in echo to her passionate storytelling.

"And then what happened?" I ask her to encourage her to keep going.

"Something changed. The world that was with the cities and the rampant war was grey and ashen. It was painted in black and white where it had been verdant green before the wars. Then, after countless years of grey ash, somebody, somehow, some way planted a flower in the wilderness. The flower grew in a beautiful field away from the cities, away from the smoke. It was just one flower but it was oh so pretty. It was yellow."

She looks up again at me before continuing her story. I find myself caught in her web of dewy innocence.

"Not right away, not at the start, but the year after that first planting, there were a few more flowers on the hill where it all started. The hill was remote, so no one came by to see them. The rains fell, and the fairies watched the crops grow of this newborn flower. Another year brought more flowers to a small patch of the hill. Another year, even more flowers covered the hillside. Soon a few humans came, took pictures, took flowers, took seeds. That was okay, even though they didn't ask permission. They grew the seeds when they were back at their houses back in the city. Those transplanted flowers grew, and more seeds were made year after year. Those beautiful yellow flowers were seen by more and more people."

She looks up again at me. She can see I have a bit of a tear now, but there is no longer a trace of sadness to her eyes, so I blink my own feelings away like a good little adult.

She gets up from my lap and goes over to the fridge. She grabs some juice and two glasses. She pours a little bit out for us and brings one glass to me. She snuggles back into my lap and drinks her own glass of juice.

"Okay. Go on, little one. I am ready."

"Then, one day, the dragons came back. Oh, they looked fierce, and they were! They remembered the war, and the pain, and stayed away from the human-filled cities. They landed where the flowers were first planted, on that remote hill. They rolled and romped around like puppies on the flower-covered hills, happy as could be that the flowers had returned to the land! Some people wanted to go back to the old ways of killing and slashing, for there were dragons! 'Fearsome brutes!' they shouted. One or two humans stood in the way and said, 'Wait! Let me go talk. Let me go touch. If they harm me, then do what you must but let me go touch. Let me go see the dragons.'

"Those first kindhearted humans went to the dragons and found the dragons weren't angry. The dragons weren't fierce, nor bloodthirsty. Not any longer. They all talked of the old days. The dragons talked of friendship and kinship that was before the hatred started. Some very few of those first brave humans were able to go high above the clouds riding a dragon. The humans who wanted to hurt, the ones who wanted to scheme, just walked away, plotting like humans do now.

"It became apparent that things weren't quite as they were and yet weren't quite as they ever will be. The ones that wanted to hurt, the ones that wanted to kill, they stayed over there, where they were all along, and the humans that wanted to be friends, the ones that wanted to ride dragons, the ones that wanted to speak of kinship, they came over here."

It was clear the girl had finished her story. She looked up into my eyes for a long moment and then put her glass down on the floor. She got up from my lap. She walked over to the light switch and flipped it on. To my surprise, the room was quite bright—a beautiful yellow and some other colours too. On the wall over from where I was sitting, there was a door I had not seen before.

She said, "You can go. It is time for you to leave and go rejoin the humans. Maybe here where we are, maybe there where some are instead. It is your choice."

I slowly stood and to her I said, "What will become of you?"

She said she would stay until she was needed again because humans can easily forget, but she remembers.

I smiled as I got up.

I bowed to her as I left the room that was dark no more, and I closed the door gently on my way out of the bright-once-more room.

The Frog

There is a thick book with yellowed pages. There is a frog too. Now, the frog is a small frog—we might say a tree frog. Green, small, and very friendly! He is flipping through the pages of the book.

I speak to him a greeting in an ancient language, and it turns out he can not only speak but can also read the words written in the book! It is a very peculiar book, on a peculiar subject. Humans would say it is written about the physics of psychic perception, or perhaps the ethereal application of physics—as I said, it is a peculiar book!

He is understanding this very, very esoteric book to a high degree of comprehension, at least based on the mutterings I can hear him occasionally utter from where I am sitting. It is a very high-level theory book, and he is understanding the talking points in the same way that some few of us might understand advanced mathematical formulas today.

He is reading the book with a smile on his face and a cup of tea at hand. When he sips his tea, his little pinky finger sticks out from the tiny teacup handle. The ornate decorations and sumptuous furniture of the parlour we are sitting in give me the feeling that a maid or a butler, as yet unseen, will come along shortly and refill the teapot and refresh the lady finger sandwich tray too. It would be a shame to get a stain on the very comfortable leather furniture, or the very expensive-looking carpet, hence why everything is served properly with a plate underneath it and a napkin beside!

The room is beautifully appointed in an outdated style, and there is a sense of old-fashioned tradition, a sense of proud craftsmanship. And I can't shake a tingle at the back of my skull, that something is unseen, something beyond seeing, that is most post-modern. There is a feeling I get as I sit watching the frog that what is old is new again and what is new is old again. As if time was somehow not linear but rather chasing its own tail. A rediscovery of that which was lost by the curious frog reading this profane book!

This little frog, yes, he understands most of the book, but I further sense he is pretending to understand that last 10 percent of it. A bravado of sorts where he may well say to anyone who will listen, "Oh, yes, I know this material well. Naturally, I do."

But he really doesn't understand because he is missing that last 10 percent. He still knows a lot, but not that last 10 percent of what the book is detailing.

The butler I expected to be somewhere close by finally comes into the room and asks, "If there will be anything else, sire?"

"No, nothing more. We will be heading out for the evening." The frog is done with the food, the frog is done with the tea, the frog is done reading the book. So the frog jumps down from the chair where he was reading and he prepares to go out for the evening.

He dons a top hat and overcoat that the butler had been instructed to bring—very proper and very popular attire amongst his peers. He starts to walk out the door. And by walk, I mean this little six-inch-tall frog is walking as any other well-heeled gentleman may do, on his hind legs!

He is now out on the city streets, just walking and greeting passersby. The greetings with his neighbours are very proper and pleasant and congenial. The frog arrives at a large home and opens the gate to the walkway. This neighbour is also well educated, but in a different discipline than the frog. Their conversations can be lively and occasionally veer away from congenial tones. This friend is someone the frog can be truthful with, someone whom the frog can banter with about heady topics that might make your head spin.

Upon entering the home's foyer, the frog starts off by telling this friend about the book he just acquired, and how the frog could understand at most 90 percent of the content therein. The friend's home is beautiful, and he has used a lot of orange, a lot of copper colours in the decorations of this home. The friend plays coy with the kindly frog, gaslighting him if you will, about the veracity of the book's authenticity and authority.

The frog is bedevilled by a gnawing sense of frustration and rising hopelessness at ever getting an understanding of that last 10 percent of the golden knowledge. So, he continues to query the unkind neighbour about how he might go about ascertaining the missing knowledge. After a few moments, the frog finally sees an old pattern of betrayal from the neighbour—a derailing of the frog's pure academic pursuit of knowledge.

Our friend the frog starts to piece together in his mind the bits of this evening's conversation that he will keep and what he will cast aside as easily as picking pickles off a dinner plate that someone has served to someone who hates pickles.

The frog wisely turns the conversation with his friend to mundane trivialities such as national news and neighbourhood gossip. A little more wine is poured, to take the chill off of the walk ahead for the frog back to his house in the cool evening air. The friends part ways.

Much like merry ole England in years past, the cobblestone streets glisten in the soft gas-lit light of the streetlamps. It is not really safe to walk these streets so late at night, but it is not really dangerous either, just to put it into perspective.

He comes around a street corner, and there is a little alcove in an alleyway, and in this alcove there is this little girl. She is about four years old. This little girl is injured. Maybe she fell. Maybe she was struck by a merciless man. At any rate, she has a nasty wound on her left foot.

The frog comes up to her and gently asks if she is alright. She is softly crying and barely able to focus on the unexpected conversation with a stranger. But she manages to say in between sobs that she is not doing very well. It turns out she had run away from home because she was mad at her mummy. Somehow in the anger, and in the running, and in the fear, and in the uncertainty of being on her own, the little girl had fallen. And now she was hungry, and the night was very dark!

The little frog that walks on two legs says to the girl, "I will if I can, and I *can* assist you! I can help you if you'd like!"

At the thought of help, the little girl starts to calm down and gains control of her sobbing. Not trusting her voice, she nods her consent for help from our friend, the frog.

Some may whisper "pedantic fellow" behind the frog's back, but he has many learnings. For example, he moves closer to the girl and sets his mind to using his often-sought-after healing abilities that he had long before ever reading the new old, yellowed book that now resides in his parlour. He is waving his hands above the sore foot of the girl. He is also using his voice, calmly talking to her of pink elephants, and sunsets, and other beautiful things to distract the wayward, scared little girl. All the while, he is working his unique healing magic on the foot that is sore.

The wound starts to shrink, and the girl reports her foot is tingling a little.

The wound is stubborn and stops shrinking all too soon before it is closed. He pauses for a moment and remembers the new old, yellowed book and the learning within. He remembers his recent conversations with his coy friend, and he tries a few things. A few things that are new. Fresh.

But his new tricks don't quite work on this wound that is so fresh. He pauses and decides to try another new approach. This new approach melds some of his knowledge with a technique that the new old, yellowed book mentioned, but it backfires and momentarily mildly increases the girl's bleeding before he reverses his course of action. He goes back to the tried and true of his old, old ways. The wound stops bleeding, and the girl reports she can feel the tingles again.

Dear readers, it certainly seems like that last 10 percent is of the utmost importance to this little girl's wellbeing!

The frog starts to stammer and feels frustrated that he is failing this girl, this girl in need. "What is the answer? How do I get that last 10 percent? How do I perfectly meld my old ways with these new techniques?" he says to no one in particular.

He takes a moment. He takes a breath. He relaxes. He digs into his heart. He digs into his intuition.

The answer that comes to him as a silent knowing is, "Don't worry about the 10 percent, don't worry about the book learning, don't worry about your friend's misguided advice, don't worry about the butler, and don't worry about this or that either."

He starts to dive into his artistry, revelling in his mind's quiet and newfound calm, and into his awareness of the girl's foot. Slowly, subtly, he starts to understand her foot, and its mechanics in significant and meaningful truths that had not occurred to him before. He applies his magic and his deep knowledge once more. That banged-up foot now starts to heal rapidly for the troubled girl, who wipes her face with her hands as a reflex to the sensation of healing.

He starts to understand the 10 percent that he was worried about—that minuscule amount that he wanted to scream about—was inside him all along! He realizes his heart is released as he moves towards the caution signs of fear and doubt, instead of away from them. This movement gels a long time coming healing within him, allowing him to grow beyond the limitation he had held on to. The little green frog starts to understand steps he can take to boldly grasp even higher levels of magic, of understanding, of love.

The frog blinks as his work subsides, and he smiles warmly at the girl. She wiggles her repaired foot, its wound all closed, and smiles back at him. Her worries have faded. In a shimmer of her own release, she morphs into a young woman of 25 years. The young woman thanks the frog and departs, though she says not where she will go next.

The frog watches her go before he turns to head back to his own house, his butler, and his warm parlour. He has a determination to write his own book.

The Cookies

There is an older man sitting at his kitchen table. He might be 40; he might be 50. He is eating a cream-center cookie. He is a cookie twister. He has twisted off one cookie from the other cookie, leaving the gooey icing center in perfect shape on one of the biscuits. He is very gingerly, very delicately, very intently eating the cookie he has.

There is a little boy at the table too, his son, who fortunately got his looks from his mother. At the moment, the boy appears to be totally starving from how he is downing the cookies by the handful and dunking them in milk as fast as he can. There are cookie crumbs and milk splatter all over the place where the boy is sitting! The son is chiding his dad for eating the cookies so carefully. Dad is ignoring the gluttony as best he can and is savouring the moment of eating, savouring the bites, and savouring the shared moment with his child. It is very much a battle of the wills.

The little kid is going, "Dad, Dad! Just, gosh darn it, dive in there and just chugga a lug the milk and grab those cookies by the handful! It doesn't matter if some crumbs hit the floor or you get milk up your nose. Mom will clean it up."

Dad responds, "No, we have to eat a certain way. We have to do it this way. This way I am eating is the nice way to do it. Very proper and polite."

So, the next morning, the father commutes to his office job—he is an accountant with a nice business suit, a nice office, a nice car. His car is a newer model and it is freshly washed, freshly vacuumed. Like I said, the father is an accountant, and he is very good with dealing with numbers, crossing the T's and dotting the I's in a numerical way.

Time passes in their lives and in this story. The son is now a teenager, with wild teenage hair, and a wildly coloured surfer shirt on. He may, or may not, smoke drugs *occasionally* for recreational purposes. Much like the boy he was, he is still messy, but now he is into video games and he is also into music. He has a job. His job is creating music for video games. But it's messy. The music he creates is messy in an unstructured way. But that melds so beautifully with video games because in games, when you make a mistake, you get a discordant sound to let you know there is a reset happening. Video games understand messy. The kid understands passion, he understands how to move and groove through the heart, whereas the father doesn't live his life like he knows that beat. The father understands logic and ordered construction of facts and figures. When the son borrows the family car, he always has to turn the radio up.

Their staid relationship has not evolved beyond the themes they explored more than a decade ago. The father is still saying variations of, "Sit up straight! Do as I do, not as you want to do!" and the son responding with his own, now-adult takes on, "You are just an old man! You don't know how to live! You are not the boss of me!" In some ways, they are peas in the same pod, for they refuse to give an inch of their small, small worlds.

We fast forward yet again in their lives. The father is much, much older now. The father lays in a hospital bed sick, very sick. The father is not gonna make it. The son comes into the stark white room, and the father can't believe his eyes. The son is now 40 years old. He's got a three-piece suit on, and he's got a fresh haircut. The son is bringing flowers from the gift shop—his father's favourites, by the way. Oh, he also has some cream-center cookies and he's got some little milk cartons like you might find in cafeterias.

He says, "Dad, Dad! Do you remember the cookies? Remember how we used to eat together?"

The father says, "Yes, I do remember. You always were so messy."

The son continues unfazed, "You were always, you know, so proper and so perfect when you were eating. I now have an office job, and a three-piece suit, just like you once did. I got a haircut, cut like you used to wear. I want to have some cookies with you, for old times' sake."

The dad says, "Okay. You gonna eat properly this time, son?"

The young man simply says, "Yes." He gingerly opens the cookie box, selects a big fat cookie, and starts to eat the way the father ate years ago ... properly and gingerly, twisting and turning, avoiding a mess.

The dad looks over at this apparent miracle and remarks out loud, "Huh, so maybe you learned a lesson or two after all." The son smiles in between bites.

And so what does the dad do? He just rips into the cookie box, grabs a handful, and stuffs a few into his mouth, and then chugs a milk carton down too. Milk splatter and cookie crumbs land all over his hospital gown as the old man lets out a thunderous burp. You can tell the father is enjoying the moment like he never quite did before, all those years ago now. He licks some of the icing off from his hands and chides his son for not getting messy. The son is stunned but manages to say, "Maybe you learned something from me too."

"Maybe I did. Maybe I did."

The Three Fires

I am standing in a large grass field with three bonfires burning close by. There are perhaps more fires in the far distance, but smoke hugs the ground like a morning fog and the crowds of people further block my line of sight. There is a warmth to the three fires as I stand quite near them. There is a comfort to the flames. There is a warm light the fires give off, but what do we—the gathered crowd and I—feed them with? What wood will we use in these warm fires as we stand around and talk of carnal things?

The first fire we feed bodies as if onto a funeral pyre. This land is scarred and trolled by war, and a war machine in full motion leaves debris to be cleaned in fire. Crunch, crunch, crunch. Munch, munch, munch.

The second fire we feed pressed logs and two-by-fours of construction lumber. The construction of much-needed new homes is paused, for the workers are now soldiers. We have the lumber but instead of building homes, we feed the fire. Wait, wait, wait. Ponder, ponder, ponder.

The third fire we place gold onto. We feed it with the gold dust of finery such as goblets and jewelry and bracelets and crowns, that turns liquid when it hits the flames. All our hopes and dreams are going up now in the warm third fire. Cry, cry, cry. Rejoice, rejoice, rejoice.

"Feed the fire! Feed the fire!" is what the gathering crowd chants as they stand around the fires. I feel a stirring of desolation inside me as the chant reaches deep into my heart for the first time. I want to keep some of those dreams, that progress, those fallen sons and daughters close by. "Feed the fire! Feed the fire!" goes the chanting, stronger now, against my will for quiet to reign. I move beyond the fire field to ease my unease. The fires three continue to burn bright well into the distance even as they recede to my occasional backward glances. I put my hands into my jacket pockets as I walk further along a path well laid, the fires' warmth now out of reach.

I walk and I walk until I come to a large stone wall. A fortification. A castle lies beyond, but the massive wooden main gate is closed. The sentries are alarmed at this stranger's approach. I ask if I am allowed to enter.

"No, no, no! Go away, good sir, or we will make your life miserable," a guard warns, but I am not myself. Not like I think I am now.

I pull my hands out of my pockets and move off to one side from the main gate. I face the stone wall and take a breath. I put my hands out in front of me and walk ahead, pushing my body through the wall of stone that is oh so big and oh so formidable. The masonry is thick, but I eventually emerge into free air, to walk unscathed into the courtyard of the fortified village, the large city gate still closed but behind me now. The townspeople are surprised at my appearance in the centre of town. The town's guardsmen go into defensive formation before me. I pause at this turn of events.

The guards shout, "Halt! You there! Stop!"

I look at them and move forward despite the danger. The men with their spears and their burnished armour hold the line of defence as I move through them unfazed and unharmed by their blades and their words. The guards have no idea what to do with a man like that. Their training is useless. Their weapons are useless, as are their shouts of control. Their shouts of authority do nothing to this man I am now. I stride with a newfound confidence and walk up the rise beyond, for the pathway to the king, to the castle strong, leads on.

The guards come up behind me, yelling at the gathered people to clear the way. The townspeople are all too happy to scatter, for the spears and armour and shouts of authority sway them greatly.

I walk alone yet surrounded by many.

The captain of the city guard riding on a horse, chestnut brown and 17 hands tall, approaches from yonder. He has on full armour. His sword at the ready, a battered shield by his side. He bellows, "You shall not pass!" through a visor uplifted. I look at him directly, I give a brief nod of respect to him, and I keep on walking. The captain has no idea what to do with a man who would go against his command, who would not obey his very stern voice. There is no charge in reply. There is no slash in reply. His mouth stays open at the sight he sees.

I walk by the horse and his rider, and the captain spurs his steed to fall in behind me as we march together towards the king.

There is a magician a little further up this path. A mage of old age, with cloak and long beard, his white hair flowing in the wind. Power, such great power, flowing all around him. He regards me as I acknowledge him in turn. He breathes a deep breath, his clenched fists relax, and his vast power stops flowing. There will be no harm from the sage, not today, maybe never again. He too falls in behind me, with the captain and the guards and the village rabble. We march to the castle. Oh, do we march!

A woman of status, a woman of distinction, comes into view as she stands by the pathway in her long dress of green with gold leaf. She is very high born. She carries a rose as she stands there agape. She tosses the rose into the path I have chosen to take. I smile a sweet smile at her sweet gesture, and 'POOF!' There appears a bouquet of one hundred roses in the hands of this lady of finery. The flowers have sweet scents, and the bouquet is presented so beautifully. As she watches me pass, she breathes in the flowers' perfume. She pauses, then turns to march alongside the mage.

The final drawbridge lies ahead, and the king's own royal guards are there with very clean capes, freshly scrubbed armour, and swords at the ready. The white marble castle glistens beyond. These guards form a formidable line—10 men deep— with their captain at the fore, his large claymore in one hand, then the other, testing its significant weight and showcasing his swordsmanship. I stop 10 paces from the captain, whose very long sword is now steady and leveled at me. He raises his sword with two hands and advances on me. The captain swings. His weapon of murder passes right through me. He fakes with a thrust, then again a slash of the polished steel sword. Furious, but with understanding rapidly dawning on him, the captain throws down his two-handed sword and steps to one side. I move to the men in the line who are blocking my way with their physical presence. They keep their places as I move among them—not hurting, not damaging, not saying a word to the guards who remain silent and baffled.

We, the mage, the lady, the captains, the guards, and I, come at last to the door of doors. This ancient, imposing door to the court is closed and locked. I pass through as before to finally witness the glorious court in all its splendour. Many beautiful tapestries and many fine sculptures are on display. The courtiers wear sumptuous clothes, each outfit finer than the next I gaze, while my nose catches the scent of exotic perfumes from far away lands. The king is on his throne, his queen beside him.

The advisors wage protest from their positions of power as the courtiers watch in silent respect. I move through them all to stand before the king. The king has a twitch in one eye as he scans his now quite crowded court before focusing solely on me. He speaks of audacity and responsibility, though his tone has curiosity running through in a kingly way.

I reply, "The people are hungry. The people need food. The people need houses."

The king protests, "The nation needs armaments. The nation has enemies." Taxation and toil are the way of the game he plays.

"The people need food and the people need clothes. The people need hope," I restate as I step one step closer to him on his high, high seat.

The court erupts as advisors renew their protests of my impudence aloud, and the courtiers relish in gossip hushed, and the guards report the intrusion I have caused. The king holds up his hand to silence those talking while he ponders what has happened today.

My voice rings out in the now silent hall, "I can teach the people how to come here unharmed. I can teach them how to walk through swords and fires bright. What would they say to you? What would they do? Your fine, fine armaments and your fine, fine castle along with your taxation and toil might come to an end if the people could walk through castles strong."

The Village

There is a fish swimming in the sea. The fish is peculiar. The fish senses a growing need inside himself. He senses he is of the fish people, and yet not of the fish people—he is one of many fish in the school, and yet aware he can leave at any time, as happy as he is now swimming in a school in the sea.

This day, this day right here and now, the fish school swims, going this way, and that way, edging closer to the shore than ever before. The one fish, the peculiar fish, separates, and yet feels the love of the school for him as he feels love for them all in turn. He rises up from the depths to spy flames, to spy smoke, though he knows not those words. He catches his breath, and breaks the waves' surface to see what he can see.

The hunters, and the destroyers of the sea, live there near the shore in the human village that is burning. The takers of lives, the scoopers of families, none return to the sea from the nets he and his kin know well. One of the human huts is burning, for it is made of leaves, and wood. He sees the hunters rushing to the water. Except they are not hunting now. Now they have buckets in hand. A line is formed by the humans, a bucket brigade, though he knows not those words. He feels their vibrations in the water, excited and strong, like when they drag nets through the schools, and through the shoals, of living flesh.

There is a desire on the fishes' parts to move towards the village, towards contact perhaps for the first time. The schools long for connection with humans, or is it peace, or is it curiosity? There was a choice the school made this day, to send one of their own—an emissary of sorts. An auspicious day to be sure, and a unique choice to select this fish above all others to be an agent of love, to be even more sure.

For this peculiar fish was willing to go, was willing to separate from the comfort of the school. There had been other fish who had, shall we say, been asked to leave the school. All the rest before had gotten to shore, and gotten a few feet, a few yards, up the sandy way. They died on the shore, not reaching the village. Our hero sees their carcasses, their bones, scattered perhaps by the birds feeding for their own gain, not understanding that the mission to connect was in love, and what they all would have gained.

This peculiar fish slips beneath the waves once again, and moves closer to the shore in the way of fish. A few of the school's members bravely swim a few meters behind him then they stop. They are uncertain of the wisdom of going closer to the terrifying chaos, when they could very well stay with their schoolmates, in the safety of the depths. As the peculiar fish starts to come ever nearer the shore, he slowly starts to morph into a land creature. As he pops out of the water, his fins turn to hands and feet, another step, and his legs and arms grow as they need to. As he walks, he becomes fish-human, with lungs, and large eyes. His skull is elongated but human enough. He retains a delicate shimmer to his flesh. He is aware that no other fish arrived on the shore that day.

Our hero arrives at the village, and now knows the names of the flame, of the smoke, of the emotions raging in the villagers, and of the bucket brigade. He understands that there are more humans than buckets. The village may go up completely, as yet another hut easily catches fire. He has a notion to squirt his stomach at the flames—his water-filled stomach.

This fish-man has an idea.

He tells the villagers in their own language of the fish in the sea, and how their guts can be filled with water. He speaks for the fish, and he speaks of hope, for there are more fish than buckets, and the fish will help the humans. The fish will help the humans if the humans open their arms at the shore. The fish would jump into the humans' arms, and then the humans would run to the flames. The fish would go squoosh, so to speak, spewing water on to the flames. "A concerted effort of teamwork would be more efficient, yes?" he innocently asks them.

A few of the villagers who heard him scratch their heads at this crazy-talking fish-man, but many villagers rush to the shore instead, hoping beyond hope that the fish-man speaks truly that there is a common bond of mutual friendship.

The fish-man was right; the fish do wish to help the humans! There is a common bond between them, but humans have forgotten it as they grew ever more gleeful doing what humans do best. The school's fish jump into waiting arms. The humans run towards the burning huts, and the flames become lessened. The humans hold hope that their village can be saved.

The flames have lessened, but there are only so many humans, and there are more fish waiting to help near the shore. The fish-man realizes that a large whale with its big stomach, could beach itself and squirt water onto this village near the shore that is still burning, and smouldering. He also realizes it would take a concerted action for the humans and the fish to help a beached whale go back into the water safely. He announces his plan to the gathered humans.

The humans vacate a spot on the beach, while some few still run buckets. The humans wait in ones and twos as the smaller fish are placed back into the ocean. A whale is called, and the nearest whale agrees. A moment later, a mighty whale comes onto the shore, beaching herself. She squirts her stomach's water to the village. The flames go out, and the danger is over.

The humans respect the agreement that was made to save their village. They fashion ropes with vines. The women make the ropes. The men make the ropes into mighty lassos. Someone remembers to put down leaves between the flesh and the vines so the tender flesh of the whale does not get cut, does not get injured—a padding of sorts. The lasso ropes are placed. The men pull, and the women pull, and the whale assists through muscles, and through fin action. The mighty whale inches closer to the water's edge.

The shoals come to the shore. A sight not seen for many a year, the fish line up with their tails towards the seashore. They start to smack the salt water into a froth that pushes the water as much as it can go up onto the shore. This assists the villagers, and this assists the whale, for they desperately need to get water under the whale again.

Some fish are on the land, and some men are in the water. There is trust, and there is teamwork. The whale is soon half in, half out of the danger of being beached. Other whales are called to assist with this rescue, and the smaller fish move aside. The arriving whales take their turns slapping the water with their flukes to bring even more water up to the beached whale. The humans clear safely out of the way, and push from the land side only.

The heroic whale finally goes fully back into the water as the humans cheer.

The fish-man stands at the shore, contemplating life of fish and humans, as he watches the celebrating villagers walk off towards what remains of their village. There will be much fixing, and repair work ahead. Two humans remain behind, and approach to ask the fish-man, "Tell us more of the great friendship between human and fish. Tell us if we can harvest our dinner still from the deep blue ocean as our grandfathers taught us. Tell us how to repay the kindness of the fish that was shown today."

The fish-man speaks before returning again to the sea. "Some few fish will come at first light to your beach. They willingly will come to be food for your families. Harvest them quickly, and mercifully, in exchange for their sacrifice. You need not go out beyond the dangerous surf to harvest anymore. Build a reef, an artificial reef of logs and stones, offshore. This would help the ocean life be abundant and strong."

The humans agree.

The Bridge

The girl looked around from where she was on a dusty dirt path. The girl looked left. The girl looked right. The girl looked down. She was at a crevasse. She sighed. She looked behind her at scrubland and boulders. She sighed again.

There was a bridge off to her left made of wood and ropes that looked sturdy enough but had obviously been there for some time, getting weathered, getting used. But by whom? She looked around and could not see another path to take. There was only one path, the path she had walked. She couldn't remember how long that had been. Forever, she supposed, as she began to play with her long hair. The path led to this derelict bridge, and the bridge lay ahead across the rocky crevasse.

She sighed again. Not wanting to go back to where she was from, she walked out onto the bridge, step by cautious step. Somewhere in the middle she tore her gaze away from the horizon, and that was when she saw a hole in her bridge. And it was her bridge, for there was no one around to claim otherwise. The hole was wide. She didn't think she could leap over it. She didn't see a way to go around the hole and she was in the middle of the bridge. There was no wooden edge to walk on. There was no tree branch to swing on, and she certainly didn't want to dangle in the air as she shimmed along using only the hand-hold rope, so she pondered for a moment. She asked out loud for help.

She got on her knees and looked closer at the hole. It was kind of ragged, like maybe something had caused it. Maybe something had ripped it out from the wood planks that the bridge deck was made out of.

Should she ask for help out loud again? She had already been given various answers in the uproarious silence of her own frantic mind. Things of the past, things of heartache and heartbreak, things that had made her cry, things that had made her stronger, and things she shied away from.

She closed her eyes. She gave thanks to the hurts she had felt many times in her past, for she had learned some harsh lessons. When she opened her eyes again, she could see that the hole had somehow filled in on the edges, just a little. She knew she had found something deep inside her that she didn't have before! She knew she had found the way to keep walking her path.

She closed her eyes again and thought about her life some more. She thought of the people who had helped her and the people who had hurt her and the people who had held her back and the people who had pushed her forward. And she gave thanks to them all in her own way. She breathed in, she breathed out in a slow, steady way and was conscious of how good that felt, and when she opened her eyes, she found rusty old railway tracks had been laid over the bridge deck.

Perplexed at this change, she blinked and looked back to where she had come from. There was no train in sight, but the tracks were there on the path she had walked to get here. The rusty train tracks were laid quite splayed and not at all trustworthy, much like this untrustworthy bridge. It looked to her as if the tracks stretched from one end of the bridge to the other end where she hadn't been yet, at least as far as she could see. She was quite puzzled at this turn of events.

She sat down on her butt and thought of the days — the days that had passed and the days forward to go. She thought of what life she had wanted, what life she had gotten, what her life could be like if she could just dream it to be.

She closed her eyes to relax, then thought on all the good stuff she had ever received and said, "Thank you, but no more of the bad stuff." She focused on the good, and she focused on the future, and she focused on what she could possibly do. When she opened her eyes, the bridge's hole was filled in slightly more than before, and the railway tracks weren't quite as rusted, splayed, and untrustworthy as they were before either. She didn't trust herself to walk on them though.

She paused for a moment. She looked up to the sky. She blinked, for the sun was bright. She got to her feet and looked over the bridge edge. It was a long way down to the crevasse. There was no way to go but backwards, back where she started. She looked up above and said, "That's where I want to be. Up above in the clouds, not here on this silly broken bridge."

She paused again and this time yelled to no one at all, "How do I get there? How do I soar with the eagles? How do I play on the clouds like a dragon above?" And she saw some new visions of her life-that-could-be, and she heard some wise words, and she knew in her heart what her future might hold. She knew for certain a thing or two she could do, and the hole filled in—now solid and steady!

She took a step back as she watched the train tracks snap into formation, straight as an arrow, down her now-trustworthy bridge of wood and rope.

She started to walk forward, a step at a time on this bridge of hers, when she heard a whistle, and she heard a train bell clanking, coming up from behind. She turned around, smiled, and waved at the conductor of the steam engine. The train was large. There were people on the train! They were laughing and joking and enjoying their day. They didn't expect to meet someone out in the middle of nowhere. And she hopped on the train, and they all continued on their way. Across the crevasse, together at last.

The Dancers

The cake is a beautiful cake. It has multiple tiers, splendid coloured white icing, with black piping and a few added coffee beans placed for highlights. It has a neighbour, a cake beside it, which in comparison is a very brightly coloured cake that must simply be a blood orange cake.

Both cakes are equally high, and both have very special cake toppers for the party goers to admire! You see, these toppers dance! One is a man. One is a woman. Each topper has their own cake. They are programmed with the energy of joy, and the energy of being skilled at dancing!

The lady dancer is lovely, and she is dancing on top of her cake, but she cannot fully showcase her moves, or dance much, as you can say that the cake top is a rather small dance floor. She does what she can, though, and she is beautiful in form and function. She is as the flame calling to a moth. She is as the pretty angel on top of the tree during holiday times. The male dancer is similarly limited to a limited dance floor, but he also does what he can with what he has available. They both appear in a monotone cornmeal colour, for that is how they were designed to emerge from the factory floor.

They are enjoying themselves, each on their cake top. He is dancing for himself, and yet he is aware of the other. She is dancing for herself, and yet she is aware of the other. They are both very aware of the audience that comes and goes, ebbs and flows around them, watching them dance on their beautiful cakes. For they are a display at a celebration, at a festival, and the cakes are beautiful and bright!

"Pablo," she calls over to him. "Pablo. How are you doing today?" she says to the other dancer.

"Estoy bien," he says with a graceful movement of his arms. "It is a beautiful night to dance!"

"We have danced before," she says.

"Yes, I remember," he agrees. He gathers himself to leap off of his cake to jump onto her cake, but there is a force field in place to prevent shenanigans like that. He is bounced back and he stumbles. He has never tried to jump off his cake before!

She looks at him concerned, but sees he is not harmed. He is just limited in what he can do. Limited to where he, and yes by extension, she, can go. She smiles a bright smile to the audience, and she resumes dancing her dance. She enjoys the rush of the moment, and she is quite beautiful, and after a moment, she smiles a soft smile at Pablo. Pablo continues to dance, not paying as much attention to the female dancer this time in his routine.

As she dances on, a new smile slowly emerges on her face. Not a fake smile for the audience, nor the earlier soft smile for Pablo. For now she knows, she knows deep inside how to bridge the gap as he tried and failed to do moments ago. She knows how to dance with her friend on his dance floor.

She opens her heart.

Her love energy gets larger, and it blossoms fully. It blossoms as a gladiola does in warm summer sunshine. The energy of her heart expands even more until it reaches across to his cake. He does not notice at first, for he is busy dancing, and busy ignoring. Soon, however, she senses that the bridge is strong enough for her to walk on, and she starts to dance across it, advancing slowly in the space between the cakes.

He does not notice at first. Pablo is busy dancing, and prancing, performing for the party's celebrants. When he turns to see what the audience is staring and pointing at, he sees her coming towards him. For a moment, for one sweet moment, he stops moving, and he stares as she dances in the space in between. He is a little fearful, and a little curious, and a little apprehensive, and a lot passion filled at what she is doing, for she is dancing quite delicately in the middle of the air, or so it seems to him. He starts to sway, and he starts to match her groove. He starts to understand how she is using her hips and senses how she will sway next in her methodical and provocative style.

He quickly matches her movements in a soft yet still somehow strong way, becoming the container, becoming the goal posts, becoming the guideline for her to come the rest of the way on her precarious journey in open space as he now knows she will. He was not at first sure if she would come over to him, but now he is sure. So he starts to call her with his body, with his dance, with his safety, with his strength.

She comes across the last few steps of open air, still dancing as though she doesn't quite believe she is actually crossing the gap between the cakes.

He starts to peacock, he starts to expand his posture, and he starts to raise his arms, welcoming her as a flamenco dancer would welcome his partner to the dance floor.

And she starts very delicately, very femininely, to dance in strong rhythm to his now-outrageous movements. Then, after a moment of delicious dance pairing, she changes her beat, slightly, imperceptibly, but he picks up on the change, nonetheless. He knows her hips, how they move, and he can tell that there's been a change, and he changes his movement to match.

He puts his hands down. He puts his hands behind his back and dances around her in a square-dancing fashion. She nods as she dances to this new dance for a heartbeat or five.

She starts to sway away, and she changes her dance again—this time into discothèque-era movements. He changes his dancing yet again, his style, his grace, and he watches her to match her, to complement her moves. No one in the now-silent audience looks away, spellbound as they are at these remarkable dancers. He knows from the heat radiating from her body, from the nights of watching her dance from afar, from the banter of her small talk and laughter when they called out to each other, how to match her, match her style. She enjoys the familiarity with her partner. She smiles quite openly at the gathering crowd, who see them dancing and are quite perplexed that there can be two dancers on one cake, for that has not happened before at any celebration. Ever.

She changes her movements again to a very formal dance, a dance popularized in French ballrooms four hundred years ago. Instantly Pablo understands and extends his hand while he bows, and she curtsies. They dance a dance that has not been seen for many generations, each knowing perfectly to step where they need to step, aware of the cake edge, aware of the onlookers, and acutely aware of each other's rising body heat.

He wonders if there is still that bridge across the gap of where his cake ends and her cake begins. He wonders if she and he can cross over to her former cake, so he starts to dance towards where she was in midair to test his theory.

She looks at him with eyes wide open, grabs his hand, and pulls him back to where she is. She is afraid now. She is concerned for him and she does not want him to fall.

But he chooses to step confidently and boldly towards his goal. The bridge is there! The bridge of her heart's making is still there, and he starts to change his dance now into hip swinging and 1960s grooving as he crosses it in style! She smiles, she claps, and she starts to dance as if in the 1960s as well. The onlookers clap as the dancers strut across the energy bridge. The dancers arrive at her former cake, and they're still smiling and dancing the 60s dance when she walks up to him, slaps his chest, and shakes her finger at him.

He stops his dancing, taps his toes, hands on his hips, and cocks his head dramatically to see what she is all about now. When she shifts into dancing the Charleston, he smiles broadly. He almost laughs out loud at the joy of it all as the dancers move into a very sensual dance. He gets his groove on and he becomes again the goalposts, the container for her, and it is a beautiful sight to see. She continues to dance this improvised Charleston with him, and he spins her away after a moment. She knows where she is. She knows what she needs to do. She starts dancing on her bridge, the bridge back to where he was and where she wasn't, and he starts to follow her, as partners do.

She shakes her head. She wiggles her finger. She stamps her foot in a very girly way.

"¡No, no, no, Pablo!"

He stops and keeps his toes tapping and his body rocking.

She dances across very beautifully, another dance that is all her own design as he claps and finger snaps to give her a tempo. She goes over the open air to his cake, what was his cake, dancing all the while. She smiles sweetly at him and she takes back her heart bloom. She closes up her heart.

He knows what she has done. He smiles, and he starts dancing as he will dance, and she starts to dance as she will dance, this time each on the other's starting cake.

Soon the music stops. She looks over to him, gives him a wink, and blows him a kiss. He bows very gracefully, very manly at an evening well spent. The audience erupts into clapping and whistles and hollers, for the dancers have returned to where they belong.

The Wall

There is a dark, dark child. A boy child that looks eerily similar to a skunk but is all black. He has some human qualities, but you would be forgiven for missing them under his magnificent black fur and how he prefers to walk on four legs, although he can certainly walk, albeit awkwardly, on two.

"I am not stinky!" the boy tells me by way of greeting me for the first time ever.

"Okay. Noted," I say to him. "My name is Morgan. What is yours?"

He replies, "Alex. I am seven years old!"

"What do you do for fun, Alex?"

Alex softly smiles, and gently takes my hand in one of his paws, as we set off to the playground! He soon enough has a game of "pass the ball" going with the other children who are there, although as far as I can tell, the rules are very ... fluid. I can hear their laughter across the field as Alex noses the ball away from one of the other boys. I see several furred children, and several human children, all playing together. I enjoy the day and I enjoy the joy of children playing. I see Alex teasing one human girl in particular, so I go over to investigate.

Her name is Maria. Her green skirt matches her green eyes, which are vibrant and shine out from her chocolate-coloured flesh tones. It turns out they often play together, and explore together, and tell each other secrets, and share sandwiches and snacks and berries and grapes—all the usual childhood-type stuff friends do. They help each other out by doing what they are best at—the girl can reach up to the tallest berry bushes and climb trees to throw apples down to Alex. Alex, for his part, has a good nose and has found many a tasty treat to share, or can easily pick things off the ground that Maria would have to stoop for—they help each other out with things of that nature. Her hands are not like his, as she has opposable thumbs. She can do things such as tying fishing lures onto fishing lines and baking sweet treats for her family, and sometimes she shares her treats with Alex too.

And they get a little bit older now in this story; they're perhaps young teenagers and they're starting to feel the first blush of puppy love towards each other. I'm being corrected. It's more than puppy love. It's the middle teenage years where it's the crush of first loves that can be so strong and life affirming.

They are both equally infatuated with each other. They're both equally wanting to be around each other, which is amazing and beautiful.

They've been hanging together as childhood friends for years and years and years and now they are going to a school dance, a community event, together as a couple for the first time. At the dance hall now, they are being very obvious for all to see—by holding each other's hands and spending time with each other—that they have progressed their relationship to be more than just friends. And a favourite song of theirs comes on, and the not-skunk boy asks the girl if she would like to dance.

She says yes, and they start to dance, and he does his best to dance on two feet. He kind of gets up on two legs, but he's a little wobbly, but he does his best. And she's just happy to be there with her friends—both human and furred, and especially with Alex, dancing to the music as teenagers do.

One of the human boys comes walking along, as for some reason he is moving through the dance hall by way of the dance floor. He knocks our poor furred friend Alex over. Instead of apologizing, the boy says, "Look, what are you doing here? You're not even supposed to be here. Get out, fur boy! You are not welcome here."

And what to do? What to do?

The furred boy tries to ignore the bully as he gets up and continues to dance with his girlfriend, Maria. There's more pushing. The bully gets one of his friends to assist, so it's two on one for the pushing and shoving and hollering on the crowded dance floor, but no one is dancing anymore anyway.

Right at the moment of truth, the words exchanged become hotter, and Alex does not know how to handle this bully, but Alex doesn't back down. He stands by his girl. They walk out together from this dance hall, hand in paw.

The bully is seething and ranting to his buddies by this time. The bully boy is very upset that this skunk boy is here with the girl, with the human girl, and lets everyone within earshot know just how he is feeling.

A few days go by, and our friends, the young lovers, are by the creek where they usually go and skip rocks and talk and not bother anyone. Except this not-so-secret spot is known by the bully, who arrives with his tagalong friends in tow.

And the bully lets our friend Alex know that he is not welcome to date this girl, this Maria. Alex has had time to think since the encounter on the dance floor and he stands up and he says, "No, I like her. I like her a lot. I will not back down."

The bully comes closer and punches him in the face, knocking our friend over. Alex lands on his back but he easily flips over. He raises his hind legs up and he kicks the bully in the chest with both legs as a horse might do. The bully receives a cracked rib or two and is now in quite a bit of pain. His friends come to life at seeing their leader fall and chase our furred friend a little bit away from the creek. The young thugs catch up to Alex, and they beat him up. The girl finds them, and Maria tries to stop the fighting. The bully followers laugh at her tears as they walk away to gather their leader up for the walk back to the human homes.

Maria says to her boyfriend, "It's not worth it," as tears start to flow freely now from her beautiful green eyes. "It is not worth it to be with you and have us together. Us being together is going to hurt you. It's not worth it."

The not-skunk takes her trembling hand, and looks her in the eyes, and says, "You are worth it. We are worth it."

She helps Alex to stand up, and he leans heavily on her. They hobble together towards his family home. His mother is quite concerned when she first sees her son in pain, and even more concerned when she hears the story of the day's events. The other furred people who live near the human part of the village are also quite upset at this incident, for the humans and the furred have gotten along for years and years and years. There has not been trouble for a long time. There are heated words exchanged between adults in both communities as the news of the fight spreads.

A sturdy wall is hastily built by human and furred alike. A line is built in the sand, so to speak. "We protect our own," is often heard out loud on many streets as the construction progresses. Life gets a little tougher on both sides of the line, for the furred did amazing work at what they were good at, and the humans did amazing things with what they were good at, and sharing it all made life grand for everyone.

The entire village was stronger when they were working together, but now they are apart. The separation is hard on Maria and Alex, though they think of each other often. They each live their lives separately but they visit the wall often, though on opposite sides of course.

Oh, they touch the wall—this wall of dirt and clay. One hand, and one paw, touch the wall every day. A friendship, and a love, like theirs is not so easy to forget and move on from. The young lovers don't know it yet, but every day they are touching the wall at the exact same spot. As time goes by, their prints sink into the wall until one day, they touch the wall's imprints at the same time together, though on opposite sides of course.

And hand touches paw for the first time in many, many, weeks.

Alex says, "I love you," and Maria answers through tears, "I love you more."

The wall, the wall of separation, crumbles before their eyes as they stand hand to paw. It collapses with a thud plainly heard by the human villagers and the furred villagers alike. The villagers stop what they are doing, they come out of their homes, they come out of their businesses, and look at the wall-that-was and look at the lovers-that-are-still.

There is some blustering from the humans standing there by their homes, but the furred are wise and they say, "Let them be! If their love can tear down a wall, then we can be friends with you again." The human women nod their heads and start to understand the situation in its fullness. One of the human men starts to speak up and talks of rebuilding the wall. His wife elbows him in the ribs, stopping that outburst cold.

The villagers cross the line that was and rekindle old friendships and congratulate the young lovers for doing what they did so naturally. They tore down a wall by touching it every day.

The Worm

There is a worm, a talkative worm. He has wire-rimmed glasses and a bowler hat that is one size too small. He and I meet travelling the same direction on a path through the grass. A path with tall green grass towering over us on either side because we are both small right now. "The grass is over our heads, and that is right," says the worm.

I take a deep breath to soak up the wonderful smells of warm earth and grass. I look up and squint at the bright sunshine filtering through the blades of grass.

"There is much to be learned in books," he says, "but I prefer adventure for my learning—a swashbuckler on the seven seas, or an astronaut in space for pretend is fine, but I prefer actually tunnelling through the ground, or even making delicious cakes, with beautiful icing. The hands-on experience is important," he finishes with a nod that puts a silent exclamation point on his remark.

I casually remark that he does not have hands.

He shrugs, or the best version of a shrug that he can do. "I have learned to live with that reality," he confides. "Other people have hands. Other people can be asked to occasionally lend a hand to one who does not have a hand."

I look at him sideways but continue walking in silence. The path gets a little denser, the grass crowds in, and we push through. There is a beautiful clearing ahead, and what looks to be huts, cottages, playgrounds—a little worm village of sorts. I see young worms playing in the playground. There are old timers in the rest home. And my friend the worm has a wife at home, greeting him as he returns to her, very affectionately, very fondly greeting him. She has food ready for a meal, and though she is a worm, she has hands. She is a worm-human—more so than he is.

She kisses her husband on the cheek and good-naturedly says to me, "Everyone has their faults," in answer to my unasked question. Her husband blushes a little, or rather he turns a little bit more amber, as is his way. She has put rather stinky food down for my friend on the dinner area, and she said she was not expecting guests, but she has some things she can put together quickly. She puts together a fresh salad for me and places it before me.

"Mmmmm," I say as a sign of gratitude at the fresh and meticulously crafted meal before me.

"Not everything is as it seems," she says. "One person eats this, one person eats that, one person has arms, one person does not. Do you wonder what we do here all day in Wormtown?" she says. Her gaze lingers on her husband as she reaches out to stroke his skin. "We do what you do. We make love, we wash dishes, we watch our children grow, we watch our parents die. We wonder what is flying around in the sky—"

"Those are airplanes," I say through my mouth filled with salad.

She quickly changes her line of conversation to, "It wasn't that long ago that there were no airplanes in the sky. How did they come to be?"

"Man invented them," I say. "Man invented heavier-than-air flight."

I notice a glimmer in her eyes, and I know she is thinking of the birds and how they invented flight much, much earlier than men ever did. I cut her off before she could voice the question I don't want to answer by complimenting the salad, on how fresh it is, and how beautiful her fine home is!

She says, "Of course it is! We grow nothing but fresh food here. Nothing is packaged. Nothing is processed—"

And I say, "What about the winter? How do you grow food in the winter?"

She nods as she admits she preserves what she can, and she says even she eats not-so-fresh food in the wintertime, but she still eats what she likes for the most part. So by the end of winter, most of the food is given over to the husband, who can eat smelly, stinky, slimy food. He blushes a little with a small smile.

"But soon enough," she says, "the food is fresh yet again. The springtime sun warms us up, and everything grows!"

"Very good," I say in between bites of salad. I'm curious. I am so curious. I am happy to be a part of this village I had never been to before. "Please continue telling me of Wormtown."

She talks of children, and she talks of laundering dirty clothes, and she talks of school, and she talks of playing. She says, "Finish up your salad. I'll take you over to the playground to show you!"

I finish my salad with a few large forkfuls.

The husband chooses to stay at home when asked if he would like to come, and so the two of us, we walk not quite arm in arm but friendly shoulder to friendly shoulder, and we come to the playground, and it is like any other playground you might be familiar with—with swings and slides and sawdust on the ground. And I notice children playing basketball, and they all have hands.

I ask, "Oh, where are the children who have no hands?"

She points a little ways away from us, and then walks with me to show me around two small hills with tunnels, places with obstacles, places with tactile objects. "The children without arms play here, each to his own."

"Do the ones with hands ever play together with the ones with no hands?" I ask.

She says, "Sometimes. They are, of course, friendly to each other, but it is ... well, how would you play basketball with someone who has no arms? The ones with hands, they could easily scoot through the tunnels, much quicker, perhaps take a short cut that those with no arms cannot take."

"So there is segregation," I say.

She searches for the meaning of this unusual word, and she finally says, "Not like you might mean. There are no different schools, there are no different playgrounds, there are no different anything. The only thing is that each does what he or she can do."

"And who rules here, the ones with hands or the ones without arms?" I ask.

"The ones with hands do things that can be done with hands, and the ones without hands do things that can be done without hands. Each is elected to their gift."

Well, that had me perplexed! I ask a very logical question, "So does that mean that the ones with hands rule?"

She replies, "No. There have been rulers without hands, but they haven't written any laws. They spoke them, they annulled them, or they enacted them, but they did not write the laws," she says with a twinkle in her eye.

"Oh," as I start to understand. "So anyone can be elected here, but the job description is dependent on who is elected."

"Yes," she says as she jumps up and down and claps. "You are starting to understand us!"

"So if a leader is elected with hands, he or she would also be expected to write the laws."

"Yes, in the law book here. There are several thick and old law books in this land. In fact—"

"And who writes the laws when there is a worm in charge?" I ask.

"Why ones with hands, of course!" She says, "Silly. Silly goose human!"

"Oh." I reflect on all this new information that is rapidly filling my head. "Just a minute. Each leader does what they do best, and anyone can be elected, yes?"

"Yes. Although we have not had many female leaders, there is one young lady who seems well suited to lead one day. When she's older perhaps she will."

"Can I go meet her? Is she available?"

"Yes!"

And we walk for a while and enjoy the pleasant day, until we see a young worm, a girl, a teenager, and she has no arms, so I know she cannot write the laws down. My friend introduces us by saying, "We have a visitor, Viola."

Viola says to me, "Hello. How are you?" with perfect grace and perfect language. I can see just in the scant few moments that we talk why she may be leader one day. She is well spoken. She is graceful. She has ideas, and yet she also listens. She is not pig headed, but she is not easily dissuaded either. Somehow, despite her having no arms, she has balance beyond her years.

We take our leave of the young lady that may be leader one day. We go up a short rise to a lookout of sorts, a little grassy knoll, and we watch the sunset.

My new friend likes to go near the water, as well, but not too close to the water because the fish and the birds think worms are for eating. I know her well enough by now that I tease her a little bit and poke her in the shoulder and say, "Well, aren't they?"

And she looks wistful, and she knows that I am teasing, but she looks far away with wetness in her eyes and finally speaks, "Many have been lost that way, including my father and mother. No! No, we are not food. Not like that anyway. Sometimes when our bodies have died, we do push them out to the pavement, to the sidewalk, to feed the birds, because there is a cycle to everything. There is a gift in giving of what was. Mama Robin deserves to eat, just as I deserve to live. I see the wisdom in that cycle."

I feel the weight of her sorrow at losing her parents at a young age. And I gently suggest we return to her house.

"Yes, that is a good idea. He will be hungry again."

I look at her and I say, "Didn't we just eat?"

And she laughs and says, "Oh, he can pack food away really good. Something to do when you tunnel as much as he does."

We come back to the house. She prepares a meal for her husband again with the stinky food, and there's a little bit of fresh greens on top, which he seems to appreciate, as we would put croutons on soup. She serves me a drink and she takes a drink for herself. We stand in the food-prep area to give her husband some peace while he eats.

"Tell me of boys. Tell me of girls."

"They are equal. Each to their gifts," she replies.

"So do the women stay home with the children and the men go and gather food here?"

"It is to each of their gifts. Generally women stay home, but they don't need to. Some are not suited for that. Some do not desire that. Some women choose to gather food, or choose to defend our village from those who would attack us. Some of the men prefer to stay home and tend to the young ones—they do not have the stomach to defend, to fight. And that is their gift. We think not ill of it here."

And I tell her of my human world, and she knows, she knows of it. And there is a sadness with her, again, a sorrow, and she starts talking about how much humans have not, for all their advancements. "Humans, they are not in life balance. They don't often put their bodies into the ground to be worm food, to be broken down. Humans often burn their dead and scatter the ashes, though not everyone does. Worms liked it better when humans were a part of the natural cycle."

"I know." I understand up to a point, so I slowly nod my head.

"And then the chemicals they spill hurt us. And they're not doing humans much good either."

This sadness, this sorrow of hers, slowly seeps into me as we talk. I yawn, then put my glass down before yawning twice more in rapid succession. I stretch my arms out and gently ask where my bed is. She shows me to the guest room. I smile because there's only one bed and the room could be used by those with hands or those without hands.

I bid them both a good night. Then I close the bedroom door and turn the light out.

The Ants

Come closer, dear ones, for story time is here! It is picnic time on a beautiful day! Yes, there is desolation all around in this sparse savannah, but the finest picnic I could imagine is laid before me! There is a wonderful blanket on the grass-covered ground, woven in a gingham style. On the blanket is a meal like no other! Amazing delicacies! Fish from Beta Centauri, fruit from Alpha Centauri, compote from Arcturus, liverwurst labelled "local," and to-die-for desserts!! Such fantastic desserts from Proxima Centauri that look beyond what you might find in the trendiest of Paris cafes! Am I alone? No, I am not.

She is there and she is sort of lying on her side, half propped up on one of her blue-skinned elbows. "It's been a while. Greetings, my friend."

There is a stirring in my heart and a stirring in my soul, for I recognize the other as a former lover and as a best friend still. We gaze at each other for a moment in quiet contemplation, and share a kiss. She giggles because that is not what she is now used to—kissing is a human thing—but she enjoys it in the same way that a human might enjoy a horse and buggy ride in a cool, quiet countryside in remembrance of what was. Yeah, the way it was. What was commonplace at one time.

There are symbols floating in the background air behind her, what I will call mathematical equations that she is thinking, even as she is talking and being with me here on the grass. This remarkable woman is transmitting her thoughts into the air all around us. I can see physically these equations; I can understand these fantastical math theorems. Well, no. I don't understand them as I am a human who avoids math whenever possible, but I recognize the floating glyphs as mathematical. I would recognize beeps and bops of a computer or a fax machine too, though I speak not their language either.

She is small talking with me, a polite conversation, about how she enjoys this sandwich, and she enjoys that cheese, and the dried fruit, and this salami. I catch her naughtily dipping her finger into the whipped cream of one of the desserts and she says she really wants to try that one later, when the time is right.

"My dear, sweet woman. My old and dear friend," said in the human tongue inside my own head as I admire her feminine beauty. But she sees my emotions, of course, in the same plain manner as I see the formulas she is working on inside her own head. And little ants are coming around now, and we're paying them no attention. Their numbers steadily increase as time moves on, but we simply brush them off the sandwiches, the treats, for we are not inclined to share our feast with interlopers. As my hand goes to brush off yet another ant crawling on my bent left knee, a heartbeat extends as time slows and the sweeping motion becomes very elongated over long seconds.

I magically morph into one of the ants, one ant of many at the human picnic, feasting at this bountiful feast in a desolate landscape. There is within me now a sense of accomplishment, a sense of pride in having found some food to share—a contribution I happily share with the tribe, the hive, the nest. These ants' tribe I am now a member of. Awareness comes flooding in, and I now know they—that is we—are building something special back at the nest! I am aware a part of me is still human, with his hand still sweeping an ant off his pant leg, yet I am also very much an ant gathering food to share with others of my ilk as I rush back to our nest to share the food freely.

I am inside of the vast ant nest now. I look up and see there is a green stalactite hanging from the ceiling at the highest point of the open space. Except it is not a stalactite. It is a creation of the ants ourselves!

It is our version of a honeycomb, our version of honey, our version of beeswax, but it is an ant version. This otherworldly structure is similar to what humans would call a light fixture. Lighting is not the function of it, but the ornate and multiple-layered structure does bring to mind an elaborate chandelier, especially considering it is hanging delicately from the ceiling. My human side is fascinated by what this could mean and asserts itself to investigate.

The ants are very reverential to this ceiling structure. It is technology of a sort no human could explain, for this mechanism is far beyond what humans currently understand technology to be. The ants move their nursery to this structure, as well as provisions for those attending this elaborate and enormous structure. On a dais at the center of this outrageous structure, there is what could be described as a being in its own right. This very unique ant is vaguely humanoid in form, and yet most definitely of the order *Hymenoptera*. Its translucent blue shell shows off a node-like thorax structure, but it has no legs attached to its abdomen, and its head is obscured by mechanisms of the machine.

This bio-mechanical humanoid of flesh and fluid, which somehow has the life essence of a higher being, a deity, is birthing the egg sack of the Chosen One, the queen ant. The sacred egg is ushered into the nearby nursery where it is cared for with the highest of care. The Queen eventually emerges from the revered single egg that the ant-humanoid deity birthed a short time ago.

This Chosen One exits her natal chamber and can already speak fluently. The other ants cannot speak as she does, but they can understand their queen. The Chosen One uses a different way of communication than the public, the masses, the general populace of the gathered ants, but they understand her via telepathy. She is speaking to the gathered ants in the nest about a grand vision, talking about a new way of doing things. She passionately talks about constructing nests in a way that the ants have not built ever before. She emphatically talks about the ants learning higher knowledge through new schools with new subjects, and new avenues of research to explore. She is not just talking in fluffy theoretical language; she is imparting new and impressive knowledge directly to her tribe mates. The vast advances she communicates in her speech in the fields of medicine, architecture, and the building trades will bring a new era of prosperity to the nest.

The Queen pauses briefly to let her words sink in. She continues her long speech by talking next about a defence force, an armed perimeter of the ants' territory as some of the other insects have not, shall we say, developed their societies beyond competition and strife. They may try to claim and disrupt this new building process of the ant nest. The defence force is not a hard line in the sand. It is more a way to protect the caravans, protect the supply lines, protect the young and defenceless ants.

She concludes her first speech by talking about using these advances to build a new tower, a new nest unlike any other ever seen on the planet. This new tower will have a certain beauty to it, and there is also a certain functionality to it. It will have balconies and ridges and levels of wonder beyond what the ants have done before.

Time goes by seemingly in the blink of an eye, and the new ant tower is nearing completion. It is tall, much taller than all but the tallest trees, and it stands proud against the harsh landscape. With a blending of technology that is old and new to the ants, the essence of higher knowledge is more easily imbued into the ant populace. The Chosen One, the revered ant queen, is no longer the only one that has firsthand knowledge of advanced topics like religion, medicine, construction, and philosophy. The tower structure allows others to be imbued with this advanced knowledge and wisdom, simply by being close to it.

And as the construction completes, the real work begins. These remarkable ants, the Chosen Ones, now plural and diversified, are teaching the many other varieties of neighbouring insects on the wide savannah new ways of assisting themselves—starting with improvements to sheltering their young.

Coda for The Ants

Excerpt from Epicsol's "The Revenant" published 12354 (new calendar)

The ants, and the rest of the insects of this mythical world, were better off because of all the knowledge that came through the first Chosen One many generations ago now. The Empires of the Insects held off on telling the humans of this beautiful world they share, the hows and whys of advanced knowledge, until the humans were ready, truly ready to hear it. There was a prophecy amongst the ants that the humans who stopped being combative towards insects are the humans who were ready to receive the advanced knowledge and share the growth of a world made benevolent. The prophecy went on to state that the humans and the insects would collaborate on majestic projects, when each was ready for the responsibility.

Over eons, the humans eventually built an even larger structure that looked very similar to the strange chandelier that the imbued ants first built in their nest way back when in the dusts of history. And those humans, in turn, had a chosen one, who turned into chosen ones, plural and diverse, which meant the humans and insects of the now-unified planet could reach out to their brothers and sisters of the stars and spread the knowledge, the esoteric abilities, that they had been imbued with.

A Note From The Author

I knew as I was writing the earliest versions of these short stories, that I was writing about "the people". Who are these people you may ask? They are us, whether they have skin, fur, feathers or claws. They are us in our magnificence, they are us in our depravity, and they are us in our struggles. I honour them in the book title, and the series name.

I chose the title of "Tuatha" for this first book as a nod to the Tuatha de Dennan of Celtic, and perhaps even older, tradition. It means "People of the Goddess Dennan." There are many competing theories of what that tribe was actually like when they lived here on Earth.

I love that modern scholars are largely faced with a mystery when researching these people, who, for the most part, are lost to the mists of time, except for oral tradition passed through many generations. These stories you have read are also based on an oral tradition of sorts, for I speak them into existence first, then lay them out in written form.

The revealing of mysteries, the spirit of life's majesty, the urge to explore unknown lands, and the discovery of hints well laid, run through the stories I wrote here.

- Morgan, July 2025

This book is dedicated to my muse.

Epilogue

I'm speaking with the girl who tells stories of long-ago friendships. You may have met her already in the prologue and again in her own story.

"Why did you sit down with me a year ago now and tell me a story of dragons and humans?" I ask her.

"I sat down with you because you came to me. I sat down with you because no one has talked to me for a very long time. There are many characters in the short stories that you present, Morgan, who don't often get talked to, who don't often get acknowledged at all. You have a remarkable way of opening doors that have not been opened in a very long time. There is a joy in talking, and there is a joy in understanding, and there is a joy in living our purposes.

"Dear, sweet Morgan, your purpose is writing stories, among other talents that will arise in good time. You knew how to access these stories; no one taught you, no one challenged you to learn this craft. No one gave you permission to experience them or to write them down. You just did it. It's not so much that I, or any character here really, am hard to find. It is that finding us is as a labyrinth, a maze, a beautiful path that not many walk—not many can walk. So you will find, dear Morgan, in the years to come, that there will be many characters for you to talk to, many stories to be told, and many rights to be wronged.

"For when you can look in the looking glass, you at once see yourself and yet you also see beyond the glass into the stories. Dear Morgan, that is a gift! I don't want to keep you, Morgan. I know you're busy and there are other characters who desire to talk to you."

Also by Morgan

The Tales of the People series

Tuatha
Fables and Parables, Morganized

The Flotsam and Jetsam series

Echoes of the Deep
Enchanted Beginnings of Love, Renewal, and
Awakening

Whispers of the Deep
Bittersweet Renewal in a Love Lost and a Love
Found

Children's Genre
Sammy the Gnat Gets a New Raincoat
If It's Sunny Out, Why Do I Need One?

Meet Morgan

Morgan Silas Donnelly is a poet, writer, speaker, and sage whose projects have been called "enchanted whimsy". His witty, wistful, and endearingly weird words often have themes of self-awareness, deeper truths, unity from chaos, and romantic love as he crafts what he calls #wordart.

His books *Tuatha, Echoes of the Deep, Whispers of the Deep*, and *Sammy the Gnat Gets a New Raincoat* provide perspectives on love and life to different ages and stages.

His poetry has been selected to be in Highland Park Poetry's summer 2025 anthology.

Morgan resides and explores in the Pacific Northwest.

Visit him online at MorganSilasDonnelly.com or @morganthewordsmith.

Meet the Cover Artist

Talia is an emerging illustrator and painter. Her style is very whimsical and magical, with an emotional flair that is instantly recognizable to her fans.

Her artwork is inspired by her inner child and her love for nature.

She can be reached for contract work through her Instagram @taliscolortouch or
email at 123talia.c@gmail.com.

www.ingramcontent.com/pod-product-compliance
Lightning Source LLC
Chambersburg PA
CBHW071018180726
48291CB00004B/1521